Loving the BILLIONAIRE BOSS DOC

dobi daniels

Luxhaven Publishing

ISBN paperback, 978-1-958987-06-3

Interior Design by Luxhaven Publishing

Cover Design by The Book Brander Boutique

Editing by JD Book Services

Proofreading by Lisa Lee Proofreading

To JC, Grandma D, and DC, whom I love more than life itself.

Dexington Doctor Billionaires Series

Loving The Billionaire Heir Doc

Loving The Billionaire Owner Doc

Loving The Billionaire Army Doc

Loving The Billionaire Cowboy Doc

Loving The Billionaire Boss Doc

Dexington Christmas Billionaires Series

A Billionaire Inventor for Christmas

A Billionaire Butler for Christmas

A Billionaire Dentist for Christmas

A Cowboy Loves the Doctor Series

A Doctor Second Chance for the Rancher (prequel)

A Doctor Blind Date for the Cowboy

A Doctor Enemy for the Cowboy

A Doctor Billionaire for the Cowboy

Standalone

Her Billionaire Nemesis (short story)

Thank you for choosing LOVING THE BILLIONAIRE BOSS DOC. I enjoyed writing the story of Gabriella Landi and Jason Silvers, two very fun characters!

It's so easy to believe you have to sacrifice your dreams to make love work or to feel that you're not deserving of love. I pray LOVING THE BILLIONAIRE BOSS DOC gives you the hope to believe that love is still possible no matter what stage you are in life.

Please continue this journey with me in LOVING THE BILLIONAIRE COWBOY DOC, which is the story about Becca, Jasmine's aunt.

You can grab your copy at
https://dobidaniels.com.

Would you like to be notified when the next
Dobi Daniels book releases? Sign up at
https://dobidaniels.com.

Once again, thank you so much for purchasing
LOVING THE BILLIONAIRE BOSS DOC and
for meeting Gabriella Landi and Jason Silvers. If
you enjoyed it, please consider leaving a review
at your favorite retailer or recommending it to a
friend.

Thanks again for your support!

Dobi Daniels

Loving the BILLIONAIRE BOSS DOC

CHAPTER 1

It all started with an anonymous call.

Gabriella Landi had decided it was a good day to ride her bike. She'd been wrist and knee deep in preparing for the Landisil-IntimiRose fashion show, and the hard work was paying off. Buyers from all around the country and a few from overseas had confirmed their attendance at the upcoming fashion show, and there was a lot of buzz in the media about the sneak peeks from the new IntimiRose lingerie collection.

But Gabriella was exhausted. A change in scenery would do her good and give her the chance to work out the knots in her back and legs from sitting down in too many business meetings all week. When she'd taken out the trash, the crisp spring air, warmed slightly by the sun, had called out to her.

So here she was pedaling down the neighborhood where she still lived with her parents. Her family's home was spacious enough for her to have her own private spaces, and any plans to move out had been shelved when her father had a stroke. But she loved the quiet cobblestone streets with tree-lined sidewalks, and she couldn't imagine living anywhere else.

Gabriella felt the stress of her week ease away as she rode beyond the familiar streets toward the busier area where the local mom and pop businesses occupied every two buildings or so. The roads were free as the streets were still sleepy at this hour, though she still took care as she rode down the narrow bike lane that ran parallel to the sidewalk.

Her phone rang.

Who could be calling her at this hour? It was Saturday for goodness sake, and the employees that worked for her knew better than to reach out except in an emergency. As the Vice President of Sales at Landisil Silicone, Gabriella believed a healthy work-life balance made for better productivity.

She ignored the call. She could always call back when she finished her ride around the picturesque neighborhood.

Her phone continued to ring.

But what if it was her mom?

Gabriella's heart quickened. Had something happened to her dad? He'd had a stroke recently and was still undergoing physical therapy. Had he had another episode? She would never forgive herself if it was the case and she'd missed the call.

She pressed the button on the wireless Bluetooth earpiece in her ear. "Gabriella Landi speaking."

"You need to pay twenty thousand dollars, or we'll release the photos," a deep, distorted voice said.

Gabriella's skin prickled, and her nostrils flared. What was this? The new scam prank in town? She didn't have time for this nonsense.

She moved to disconnect the call.

"Don't cut the call unless you want everyone to know you wear an undersized black and white polkadot bra with white granny panties."

Gabriella's breath caught, and she almost lost control of the bike. She'd worn the combination a few weeks ago when she'd been in a hurry to get to her destination—the black and white polka dot was an old comfy bra she'd liked in the past but rarely ever wore these days.

How was it possible a picture of her had been taken in it? What was going on?

"Deposit twenty thousand dollars in the next twelve hours, or your pictures will be released on the internet for the world to see," the voice said harshly. "You should receive a message with an account number and a photo in case you think this is a joke." Her phone pinged. It had to be the message. "Don't call the cops, or the photos will go out. You have twelve hours. The clock starts ticking now." The line went dead.

Gabriella's heart pounded so loudly against her rib cage she was afraid it would burst through. She couldn't think—her brain seemed to have shut down.

"Watch out!"

Gabriella looked up to see herself careening toward an old lady crossing the road right ahead of her, who seemed oblivious to her surroundings. Gabriella pressed the brakes to slow down, but it wasn't enough. The old woman was coming up too close!

Suddenly, strong arms grabbed her handle bars and steered them toward the sidewalk. The bike swayed and then collapsed, and Gabriella found herself landing on a solid mass of muscle. The darkest pair of brown eyes she'd ever seen stared back at her. There was something familiar about them, like she'd known them a long time ago, though she couldn't remember where or how.

"Ma'am, are you alright?" asked a beautiful baritone voice that made her heart skip a beat.

Her face grew warm, and she scrambled off him. "I'm so sorry ... thank you ... I didn't mean ..." She looked to see the old lady had made it safely to the other side of the road. *Thank goodness.* Then she turned back to her savior.

The man, who looked to be in his early thirties, got up and dusted the beige spring trench coat he wore over his suit. He could very well have been a model for a high-end men's magazine with the effortless way his clothes framed his body. Gabriella was still a sucker for good-looking, well-dressed men, though she'd learned her lesson not to judge a book solely by its cover.

"Are you alright?" he asked, the hint of a British accent coming through. It was just her luck. Why did she have to encounter her deadliest combination today? Who wouldn't swoon at a gorgeous man with a British accent?

Gabriella took a deep breath and adjusted her helmet. Who was she kidding? Regardless of the instantaneous attraction, nothing could come out of associating with this man—she'd been burned too many times. A man's beautiful face didn't mean he had a beautiful soul. It was time to go her way, though a part of her yearned to stay and talk with him while admiring his handsome features. "Yes, I'm fine. Thanks for your help."

She picked up her bike. It seemed to have survived the encounter just fine. Then she noticed the man was rubbing his wrists. "Are you okay?"

"I'm good. It's nothing." He dropped his hands into his coat pockets. "I have to go." He gave her a warm smile. "Take care."

The man turned and walked away.

Gabriella stood there and watched him leave.

She was grateful for his help, and the encounter with him had been a welcome distraction that had made her forget the blackmail. For a second.

She let out a sigh. Now she had to deal with it.

She glanced back at the guy as he disappeared down the street, and Gabriella hoped his wrists were alright.

CHAPTER 2

Jason Silvers' forehead creased in concentration as he continued the breast reduction surgery for the patient lying in front of him on the operating table. Beth Moore, a forty-two-year-old professor, had presented at his clinic with disproportionately large breasts that were causing her chronic neck pain, back pain, and skin irritation. Given that breast surgeons at Dexington Medical were booked out six months ahead, Beth had been lucky to attend Jason's first clinic at Dexington Medical after his move from Connecticut. She'd gotten a spot on his schedule a month later.

The first two hours of surgery had gone off

without a hitch, just like he'd expected. The surgery would have taken much longer, but Jason had lost count of the number of times he'd performed this surgical procedure and could probably have done it in his sleep. Besides, the breast reduction in this case would only take Beth Moore down two bra cup sizes. The more changes in cup size, the longer the surgery tended to be.

Jason accepted the suture from the scrub nurse. Time to finish up and be done.

As he leaned forward to install the first stitch, Jason's hands trembled.

He glanced sharply at them. For as long as he could remember, his hands had *never* shaken during surgery. Sure, tremors could happen if he was tired or exhausted, but Jason was fastidious about providing the best patient care and gave each surgery his best. He'd usually sleep the night before and eat a light breakfast the morning of to prevent possible tremors from fatigue or a low blood sugar level, and he'd done the same for this surgery. So what could possibly be the problem?

He attempted the stitch a second time, and his hands shook even more.

Jason's heart pounded. What was going on? He had a patient under general anesthesia, and he couldn't afford to waste any time.

"Dr. Silvers ..." It was Lisa Shucks, the fourth-year surgical resident, who was assisting him on the procedure. She must have noticed what was going on. Jason had worked with her on a few surgeries over the past month and found her very competent and intelligent. He could trust her to finish up the surgery well if required, but Beth Moore had been concerned about possible scars on her breasts from the procedure, and the ability to keep those minimal came with experience, something he had plenty of. He'd given his word, and he intended to keep it.

"It's fine, Dr. Shucks." He had to try one more time. *Come on, Jason. You can do this.*

Jason gripped the forceps and said a quick prayer before taking a deep breath. Cold air filled with a mixed aroma of sweet-smelling gas anesthetics and antiseptic scent rushed into his nostrils.

He leaned forward and sutured the first stitch. This time, his hands remained steady.

His shoulders relaxed. *Thank you, God.* Since

he'd found his rhythm, Jason focused on finishing the stitching as quickly as he could. Twenty minutes later, the surgery was over, and Beth Moore was on her way to the recovery room.

Jason stripped off his surgical gear and mask, washed his hands, and headed out of the OR.

The surgery had been successful, but what had happened back there? As a physician, he might have dismissed it and chalked it up to tiredness, but as a surgeon he had to pay attention. His hands were his greatest tool and meant everything to him. Time to get a check-up to make sure everything was alright.

But he had a feeling something was wrong, and things could never be the same again.

Jason had reached out to a colleague in the Orthopedic Surgery department through whom he'd gotten an appointment with Dr. Meade, the leading hand surgeon at Dexington Medical. Dr. Meade had ordered some tests, and now Jason sat in his office waiting to hear the results. Hopefully, whatever was wrong wasn't serious.

"I'm sorry, Dr. Silvers," Dr. Meade said, his startling blue eyes connecting with Jason's.

Jason froze, and sweat broke out on his forehead. No, it couldn't be terrible news. It just had to be Dr. Meade's communication style. Deliver the bad news and then the good news, right? *Everything is alright,* he told himself.

He swallowed and straightened his shoulders. "What is it, Dr. Meade?"

"The MRI results showed there was some recent damage to your ulnar nerves. The trauma you had a month ago shouldn't have been enough to cause significant long-term damage. Unfortunately, you've had previous injuries to your wrists before, correct?"

"Yes," Jason said. It had been from playing polo in his early twenties. He'd enjoyed the sport but had dropped it once he'd noticed the impact on his hands.

"Well, it seems you had some residual damage from those injuries which were now complicated by the recent trauma."

"But why didn't that show up when I had my wrists checked out after the bicycle incident?" Jason asked.

"Do you have the MRI from that visit with you?"

"I'd have to request it from the hospital in Connecticut."

"We can review that for you whenever you receive it." Dr. Meade picked up the MRI in front of him and shared it with Jason. "See here? The damage to your right seems to be worse than the left."

"Does that mean—"

"Yes, there is some hope we can get the left ulnar nerve to function fully again with extensive treatment, but unfortunately we think the right ulnar nerve is permanently damaged, and the fine motor skills of that hand won't be fully restored—not to the level required for surgical work—even with the best treatment available. But it would be more than adequate for everyday life. I'm so sorry, Dr. Silvers."

Jason squeezed his eyes shut before opening them again. Why did it have to be his dominant hand? "What about surgery? Can't it help?"

Dr. Meade shook his head. "I think it would be counterproductive in this case. You might even lose some of the function you have right now."

"So there's nothing I can do."

"Not at this time, nothing short of a miracle."

Jason felt like a boulder had landed on his chest. No surgery? It was like saying that his hands had been cut off! He loved his work and his patients. Did it mean all his hard work and the years of training he'd endured had been in vain?

This was all he knew. Starting life over in his thirties wasn't in the plan when he'd moved to Dexington. Why did he have to be punished when all he'd done was save an elderly lady from being hit? He didn't regret it—a life could not be compared to his hands. But still, he wished this had not been the result.

"Are you alright, Dr. Silvers?" Dr. Meade's voice brought him back to the present.

"Yes … yes, I'm fine." What else could he say?

"I'm sure this is a big shock. Why don't we start with the treatment plan and go from there? Who knows? Miracles could happen."

"Yes, maybe." He couldn't imagine receiving one.

"Why don't I pencil you in for next week and we'll go from there?"

"That's perfect." Jason said in a calm voice, when all he wanted to do was run to the bathroom and throw up.

Dr. Meade typed into his computer and then turned to Jason. "Okay, I'll see you next week," he said.

Jason got up. "Thanks for your time, Dr. Meade."

"You're welcome."

Jason held himself ramrod as he left the office and headed down the hallway. The patients and medical staff heading off in different directions paid him no attention. Once he exited the clinic area and rounded a corner, he collapsed against the wall. His body trembled, and he shut his eyes.

How could this have happened to him of all people? He'd accepted most of the other decisions forced upon him by his parents, social circle, and society. But working as a breast surgeon had been the one thing he'd ever insisted on for himself. The joy he derived from it had given him the strength to endure everything else, and now it was gone.

He slammed his fist against the wall behind him. Why did it have to be this? He could have lost all the money he had—which ran into billions of dollars thanks to his family's old money and his parents' savvy investments—and he would have come out okay as long as he was still a surgeon. But with the loss of his ability to operate, his life seemed to have lost all direction. Jason had no idea how his heart was going to survive this shock. What was he going to do now?

"Hey, Jason, are you okay?"

He opened his eyes to see his best friend, David Landi, standing before him with a concerned look on his face. David was an attending like Jason at Dexington Medical but had specialized in reconstructive surgery. David had reached out to Jason once he'd returned stateside from his stint in the Army and was the reason why Jason had transferred from Connecticut to Dexington Medical.

They'd met in a summer camp as kids and had been best friends ever since. They'd always talked about working together, so when David had returned, Jason had figured it was a good time as any. He preferred the slower pace of life in Dexington, yet it was close enough to Connecticut, New York, and Boston that he could hop to any of those cities whenever he wanted. His parents had been against the move, but the fiancée his parents had chosen for him hadn't cared, so Jason had packed up his life and changed cities. In fact, he'd been on his way to the job interview at Dexington Medical when the incident that damaged his hands had occurred.

Jason shook his head in response. He wasn't fine. How could he be when his life had just turned upside down?

David swung his arm over Jason's shoulders. "Let's find somewhere quiet to talk." He led Jason into a nearby empty conference room and shut the door behind them. Then he turned to Jason. "What's going on?"

Jason slumped into one of the swivel chairs that surrounded the long rectangular table in the center of the room. "I'm screwed."

David grabbed a second chair and pulled it beside Jason's. "What is it? Tell me."

Jason loosened the tie around his neck. "My hands are damaged, David. How am I ever going to perform surgery again?"

"What are you talking about?" He glanced at Jason's hands. "They look fine to me."

"They're not. I hurt them the day I had the interview here with the department chief. I saw my doctor when I got back home in Connecticut, and everything seemed fine. But my hands shook for the first time during surgery earlier this week. It was bad, David. I don't know how I even managed to finish that surgery. I was afraid it would happen again, so I got an appointment to see Dr. Meade. You know him, right?"

"Who doesn't? He's a star around here. What did he say?"

Jason shot up from his chair, walked over to the window, and looked down into the busy street below. Everyone seemed to be going about their normal business. Was he the only one that felt desperate? "My ulnar nerves are damaged, the right worse than the left. With treatment, they can get the left back to normal, but he thinks that won't be possible for the right, which means I'll have a hard time performing surgery, a risk I'm not willing to take with a patient's life on the line." He ran his hands through his hair. "What am I going to do now? Being a surgeon was all I ever wanted."

David got up and walked over to where Jason stood. "I know. I got interested in surgery because of you. It's all you ever talked about. All the time."

Jason glanced at him, allowing a small smile to grace his lips. "Sorry about that." Then the smile disappeared. "Now we won't even get the chance to work together. That dream has gone down the toilet. I can't believe it's over before it started. My life is over."

"Don't say that. I'm sorry about what happened to your hands." He threw an arm around Jason's shoulders. "Don't worry, old friend. We'll figure something out. Together, okay? And who knows, a miracle might happen."

A miracle? Jason doubted that it'd ever happen to the likes of him. He'd been blessed with enough money to last him many lifetimes over. Wouldn't it be greedy of him to expect a miracle as well? But Jason gave David a faint smile, though his heart remained full of grief. "Okay."

They both turned back to the window and quietly looked out into the street for many long minutes.

Jason let out a sigh. Would his life ever have meaning again?

Gabriella Landi's hand trembled as she replaced the receiver back on its cradle. How dare he call her on her office line! Her executive assistant had said the call was from a client, so she'd taken it in the midst of a busy Monday morning.

As Vice President of Sales at Landisil Silicone, she was typically always busy, but her work had doubled with the launch of the Landisil-IntimiRose brand. Gabriella couldn't remember when she'd last had a decent night sleep and had been looking forward to having a stress-free evening. Then the blackmail call had come through, asking for double what she'd been giving him. She had no choice but to pay him what he wanted, but that didn't mean she was happy about it.

She pulled her desk drawer open. It was chock-full of sweets and chocolate. She picked one up and popped it into her mouth. The sweetness filled her oral cavity, and she felt her anxiety from the call ebbing away.

Gabriella let out a sigh. Thinking about the call wasn't going to get her work done, and there was still so much of it to take care of.

There was a knock on her door, and her executive assistant, Lacey, peeked in. The attractive brunette was wearing her signature pink glasses, which she pushed up the bridge of her nose. "It's time for your meeting with Hank Foster," she said.

Gabriella looked at her in surprise. "Foster? I thought I had a meeting with Sanchez." Sanchez was Foster's direct subordinate, and the one who did all the actual work and knew the numbers. Given that Gabriella and Foster never got on well, Gabriella preferred meeting with Sanchez and only touched base with Foster when she had no other choice.

"My bad," Lacey said. "Sanchez called and said he had to travel out-of-town for the next three days, so Foster was going to come and see you instead."

Gabriella ran her hands through her dark wavy hair. Just when she'd thought the day couldn't get any worse. She didn't have the emotional bandwidth to deal with Foster today, but she couldn't cancel the meeting. She had a major project, SK101, that was going to start soon, and she needed to ensure that the finances for the project still worked from the last time they'd discussed it at the board meeting.

"Send him in," Gabriella said wearily.

"Are you sure? You don't look okay. I can postpone the meeting if you like." Gabriella and Lacey had grown close after Lacey joined the company three years ago. Lacey's bubbly personality made her easy to like, and she was a fabulous assistant and an effective gatekeeper.

Gabriella waved her concern away. "I'm fine. Just a little tired."

"Okay, I'll send him in."

Gabriella smoothed down any stray strands of her hair as she waited.

Hank Foster stepped into her office a few seconds later. Tall, with a wrestler's body build, he looked more like a mob boss than the CFO of a billion-dollar company. "Miss Landi," he said.

Gabriella cringed. Everyone at the company called her Dr. Landi since she had a PhD in materials engineering in addition to an MBA. But Hank insisted on calling her Miss Landi as if it was beneath him to acknowledge her accomplishments and to remind her how old she was. Not that twenty-eight years was anything to sneeze at, and she'd worked very hard for most of those years. Her older brother and only sibling, David Landi, was a genius, and Gabriella had tried hard to keep up with him.

Her efforts had paid off, which was one of the reasons she occupied this seat and was being considered for the CEO position now that her father was retiring. Her brother had founded Landisil Silicone and then handed over the reins to their father to enable him to focus on his career as a reconstructive surgeon. Working alongside her father, Gabriella had watched him grow the company into what it was today, but his recent stroke had him considering an advisory role like David had.

Gabriella was excited about the opportunity, but Foster seemed to be angling for the same job and was determined to do whatever it took to make it his spot. Knowing him, he would try to keep her off balance with this meeting.

"Please sit," Gabriella said as she gestured to the visitors' chairs.

Hank sauntered over, pulled back one of the chairs, and dropped his frame into it. "We need to talk about the SK101 project," he said.

"I'm assuming our numbers still work for it."

"Well …"

Gabriella frowned. Foster always did this, keeping her in suspense when a simple yes or no would do. "Look, I need to know if we're still on-track with the finances for the project."

Foster leaned back in his chair and crossed his legs. "We are, with a little caveat."

What trick was he trying to pull? She really didn't need this. "What's it now?"

"We had to use some of the funds to support the Landisil-IntimiRose brand launch."

"I thought a separate set of funds had been set aside for that."

Foster gave her a look as if he'd just fielded a question from a child. "True. But that was before the market took a dip last month, and the value of the invested funds declined a bit. You know how volatile it can be sometimes."

"But it should still be enough. We included a buffer in the budget for this reason."

A look of annoyance crossed Foster's face, and he uncrossed his legs. "We have to remain cautious, since we don't know whether there will be more volatility in the near future. It's better to err on the side of caution and make sure we have enough liquidity at all times."

Gabriella fought the urge to reach across and tweak his long nose till he came to his senses. Did he think she didn't know the company had put aside hundreds of millions of dollars for emergency purposes? Landisil Silicone had done well in recent years and had a robust balance sheet, which supported its policy to keep as little debt on the books as possible.

But her hands were tied now. If she didn't accept his terms and decided instead to take the matter before the board, Foster with his gift of gab could sway the board to his side, and Gabriella didn't want to have to invoke her family's rights as owners of the company just to stop Foster.

It was simpler to just go with the flow for

now and then report him to the board if he put any further roadblocks against her. SK101 was very important to the company—its projected ability to increase the company's sales figures by twenty percent meant more profit for the board. "So what do you have available for us?" Gabriella asked.

"Forty percent for Phase One."

The devil. He'd managed to skim right around the bare minimum they needed for the first phase. Was this his way of keeping them on a tight leash so that she was forced to return to him for any minor budgetary changes? Thankfully, she'd insisted that Sanchez be listed as the finance department's point-of-contact for the project. He'd be the one, instead of her, that would have to deal with Foster for any budgetary changes. Gabriella doubted Foster knew she'd included that as a key requirement when the board had signed off on the project. She'd had a feeling Foster would try to undermine her, so she'd insisted on Sanchez's name as a precaution. She could live with this for now. "Okay," she replied.

Foster's eyebrows arched in surprise. "That's it?"

Gabriella got up and gave him the sweetest smile she could muster. "Thanks for coming in. I won't take up any more of your time."

Foster's face hardened as he rose to his feet. "You won't get the CEO position," he said.

Ah, finally! He'd let out what he'd really come here to say. But she'd already made up her mind not to address the topic. "Have a good day, Mr. Foster," she said.

Foster glared at her one more time and then stormed out of her office.

Gabriella collapsed into her chair once he'd left. She felt drained of any energy she'd had remaining before Foster showed up. Sadly, she still had a lot of work to take care of.

She let out a sigh. Today's work was already a lot. It would only grow worse once the SK101 project started. Thinking about it was already giving her a headache. She pulled open her desk drawer and popped another sweet into her mouth.

Maybe it was time she either expanded her team or got someone to take over some of the load. But that couldn't happen today, so she still had to be the one to take care of everything on her plate. It was time to focus on what was before her if she had any chance of leaving today.

Her office line rang. Gabriella looked at the displayed number and pressed the answer button. "What is it, Lacey?"

"David would like to see you in his office."

David was here? He hadn't told her he was coming. And why hadn't he dropped by her office first like he typically did?

Gabriella jumped to her feet.

Time to find out what David was up to.

Gabriella pushed open the door to David's office and stepped in. He'd given her free rein to decorate his large corner office, and she'd done it up in masculine blues and browns. She loved how warm and comfy it'd ended up. But chatting with her favorite person here was what made it extra special.

David had been the most important person in Gabriella's life until he'd shut her out after the death of his ex-fiancée and disappeared to Germany to work for the Army. Gabriella had felt like a ship without its anchor during the years he was gone, but she'd also grown and learned to be independent. She was glad he was back, and that their relationship had been reestablished. She even had a new family-member-to-be in the form of her childhood friend, Jasmine, who was now David's new fiancée.

Gabriella was glad that David and Jasmine had found each other again after all the years. Observing their love, she sometimes wished she had a relationship like theirs. How wonderful would it be to have a man who loved her whole-heartedly? But Gabriella wasn't foolish enough to believe it could happen for her. Their love was special, the kind that was one in a million.

There was only one person she'd ever thought it could happen with, but he'd never once looked at her that way, even though he'd treated her well. In his eyes, she'd only been the kid that followed him around. Life had taken them in different directions, and that had been the end of it. She only ever thought of him any time her relationships failed, and she was down in the dumps. But she put him out of her mind once she came to her senses. Wishes were only dreams, and Gabriella had to live in reality.

"Hi, Ella." David's voice pulled her back to the present. He was dressed in a blue button-down shirt with the sleeves rolled up and grey slacks. Considering how much buzz his presence at the office created, Gabriella was just glad he came by occasionally. It was already bad enough that office productivity went down each time he stopped by, with all the ladies vying for his attention, though they clearly knew he had a fiancée.

"Hey, David." She moved to where he stood and gave him a hug.

David held her away and examined her face. "You look tired."

She gave him a warm smile. "I'm okay."

"I don't think so. I know how good and competent you are. You must have too much on your plate for it to affect you this way."

"I can handle it."

"I know you can, but I don't want you to. You're my only sister, and I need you to be alright. I don't want you run to the ground like Dad was. Besides, the SK101 project is going to start soon."

"Don't worry. I'll be fine."

"Well, I decided to do something about it." A smile teased at the corners of his lips.

A feeling of unease swept through Gabriella. What had David done? The last time she'd seen this look on his face was when he'd done something she was absolutely horrified about. "What do you mean?"

"I found someone to step in as President of the Landisil-IntimiRose venture."

Gabriella was grateful if it was just that. It would allow her to focus on the SK101 project and the other plans that would position her well for the CEO job. "Who? Someone in the company?" Anyone was fine as long as it wasn't Foster or one of his lackeys.

"Someone from the outside."

Gabriella's shoulders relaxed. This was even better. A neutral party who would not be sucked into the company politics, at least not at first. But why did she sense that was not all? "Anything else I should know?"

"Well …"

"Just tell me what you did."

"I might have also told him he had a shot at the Landisil Silicone CEO position."

Gabriella stepped away from David. "What?"

"I'm sorry ..."

"How could you? You know fully well that the position is mine, David. I worked my tail off for this, even when you disappeared."

A flash of pain crossed David's face, and Gabriella felt bad for mentioning the incident. It had happened right after David's ex-fiancée died. David had cut Gabriella and the rest of the family off at the time, and he'd regretted every minute of it.

"Gabriella, I'm sorry," David said. "I thought I was helping. You used to be so fun-loving and had big dreams of traveling around the world. I feel like I tied you down with this job. I thought you should be free to do whatever you wanted with your life."

"I was young then," Gabriella responded. "This is my dream now. You had no right to make any decision on my behalf. You should have talked to me first." Well, David had every right since he owned about seventy percent of the company, but still.

"I'm sorry, Ella. I truly had no idea. Do you want me to tell him the offer is off the table?"

"And ruin your reputation in this business?"

David came over and gave her a hug. "Thank you."

Gabriella tried to wriggle her way out of his arms, but David held fast. "Let me go," she said.

"Can't I hug my little sis any longer?"

"Go hug Jasmine if you need one." She was still mad at him.

David gave her a kiss on the forehead before letting her go. "That's an idea. Maybe I should go look for her right now."

"And let everyone at the hospital keep gossiping about how she managed to snap up the hottest attending around?"

"Is that what they're saying? I'm that handsome?"

Gabriella chuckled and hit his arm. "Oh, stop it with your vain self."

David grinned. "It's good to see you smile again. And I'm really sorry about the CEO position."

"I still have a chance. No one is going to take it away from me."

"And who knows? A healthy competition might not be so bad."

"David—"

He lifted his hands in surrender. "My bad."

"So when do I get to meet him?"

David looked at his watch. "He should be here by now." There was a knock on the door. "That should be him." Then in a louder voice, David said, "Come in."

She turned as the door opened, and David's new hire stepped through.

Gabriella's world turned upside down.

CHAPTER 4

Gabriella's eyes widened. It was the man from the bicycle incident! How in the world?

"Hi, David," said the same baritone voice she remembered, the sound stirring her insides. "Is this a good time? I can come back if you prefer."

"It's fine," David said. "Come on in."

Gabriella was still staring as the man entered the office and shut the door behind him. She had to admit this guy looked good in whatever he wore—the custom grey sleek suit he was in accentuated broad shoulders she would gladly rest her head on.

David stepped forward and gave him a bro hug. "Hey man, how are you doing?"

"I'm good," the gorgeous man responded. Then his eyes widened when he noticed her. "Oh, hello."

So he remembered. Thank goodness she was more put together than the last time he'd seen her, all dressed up in a gorgeous black three-piece suit with fitted pants that stopped just above her ankles. She looked great if she said so herself.

"Hi," she responded with a slight tremor in a voice.

Her cheeks warmed. What was wrong with her? He was just a guy for goodness sake.

David looked from the man to her. "Oh, I see you two remember each other!"

"Sort of," Gabriella said. She hadn't told David about the bicycle incident, since he'd want to know what got her distracted in the first place. Gabriella had decided to hide the black-mail from her family, and it had to stay that way.

"We met briefly on the street," the handsome stranger said.

David laughed. "You don't remember each other?"

Gabriella looked at the man in confusion.

Was she supposed to know him? His eyes still felt familiar, but other than that, nothing else came to mind.

David shook his head. "Unbelievable. Gabriella, this is Jason Silvers, my best friend from summer camp, and the new President of the Landisil-IntimiRose venture. Jason, this is my little sister, Gabriella, Vice President of Sales here."

Wait, hold on. This stunning hunk was Jason Silvers? *The* Jason Silvers that she'd had a crush on when she was much younger, the same one she'd followed around when he'd spent the summer with them in Dexington in his last year of high school? They'd lost touch when he'd headed to Europe for college. No wonder her heart had remembered him, even though he'd gone from the gangly teenager she'd known to God's perfect creation.

But Jason's face paled instead. "This is Gabriella?" *Wait a minute.* Wasn't he happy to see her?

"Yes," David responded. "One and the same. Remember how she used to follow you around?"

"David ..." Gabriella warned.

"Sorry. It was funny and cute at the time."

"Nice to see you again, Gabriella Landi." Jason extended his hand for a handshake. He seemed to have recovered from whatever had been on his mind.

Gabriella accepted the handshake and felt a surge of electricity pulse through her arm at his touch. She quickly dropped his hand. Why was she reacting this way? Sure, he was her one-time crush and a really good-looking fellow. Unfortunately, he was now also her *competitor*, fighting against her for the CEO seat. This was not the time to make friends.

She allowed a bland expression to fall over her face. "Welcome to Landisil Silicone," she said.

"Thank you, Gabriella." The sound of her name on his lips woke the butterflies in her belly, and her breath hitched.

She shot her brother a dark glare and wished she could just whack him on the head. Why did he have to bring in Jason of all people as her competitor? He'd managed to turn her Good Samaritan into her enemy. Because that was what he was, as long as he was gunning for her CEO position. Now, she didn't know whether to thank Jason for saving her the last time or drive him away from Landisil-Silicone.

How was she expected to compete against him while fighting her attraction to him at the same time?

CHAPTER 5

Jason couldn't believe the lady standing in front of him, the one he'd saved, was his best friend's little sister. She was no longer the cute little kid that had followed him around most of the summer when he'd been here many years ago. David had thought her annoying at the time, but Jason had been entertained by her antics, which had been the perfect distraction from the arranged engagement his parents had roped him into. It was the primary reason he'd run away to Dexington.

But it would have been better if he'd saved a stranger in the biking incident. How would she feel if she realized she was the main reason he couldn't operate anymore? The last thing he needed was the kid who'd brought sunshine to his life many years ago to become guilt-ridden. He'd have to make sure she never found out.

He thought back to how she'd made a difference for him. Gabriella had no idea she'd helped him stay sane in the craziness that was his family life. Even though Jason had always known his parents would want to plan every aspect of his life and had accepted it as the price to pay for being born into such extreme wealth, he'd still hated every minute of it.

There had been no alternative except to go with what they'd arranged. Anyone who'd rebelled in his social circle had paid dearly for it one way or the other.

Besides, he'd seen enough to know that marriage wasn't all it was made out to be. Folks he'd known who'd even claimed they were madly in love ended up at each other's throats a few years later. And his parents' marriage was no better—sometimes he wondered if they even liked each other.

So, fighting his parents' choice hadn't been

worth it. His mother would kill him before she allowed him to ruin her reputation. The girl in question had seemed decent compared to most in their social circle, so he'd accepted it for what it was.

Still, it had been a little hard to accept, so he'd run away to David's house to clear his head. Gabriella had been a ray of sunshine in his bland world, and he'd appreciated and enjoyed her presence more than she would ever know. She'd been only a few years younger than Jason, and David must have noticed Jason liked her, because he'd made it clear that Gabriella was off-limits. He assumed it was still the same way now.

But Jason hadn't expected her to morph into the beautiful woman that was standing in front of him. She was most likely in a relationship—there was no way guys would have left her alone.

Not that he should be concerned about her relationship status. He had a lot on his plate right now with dealing with his damaged career.

Sure, he wasn't in a relationship anymore since the ice princess he'd been engaged to—yes, he'd found out over the years that she wasn't quite the quiet girl he'd thought her to be—had broken it off in a huff as soon as she'd heard Jason was no longer able to operate. He had no idea how she'd heard about the injury—maybe she had someone keeping tabs on him—but he'd been relieved to be free of her and disappointed that it was all that had mattered to her.

Now, he didn't need a new relationship. He had to come to terms first with the death of his surgical career and then find new direction and clarity on what to do with his life going forward.

He had time to do that. Jason had taken a one-year sabbatical from the hospital, and his department chief had been understanding and signed off on it. If his hands weren't fully recovered by the end of the leave, then he would have to resign. Jason planned to make the most of the time by focusing on his treatments and exploring this new career opportunity that David had handed to him.

Still, David had encouraged him not to give up, but just to do the best he could, and leave the rest to God. Jason didn't have a strong faith like David's, but he was willing to believe that some good could come out of everything.

Best of all, he was grateful he had a friend

like David who could hire him into a good position without questions. Jason would have had a much harder time dealing with the loss of his career if he didn't have something to occupy his mind.

He wasn't interested in running a hedge fund or going into politics like his parents would have preferred, and the job at Landisil-IntimiRose was close enough to the world of breast reconstruction to keep him intrigued. So what better way to show his appreciation for his friend's support than to keep the promise he'd made to David many years ago and consider Gabriella a colleague only.

"Oh, one more thing," David said.

What other surprise did David have up his sleeve? He glanced at Gabriella but couldn't read her expression.

David leaned against his desk and folded his arms across his chest. "Jason, since you are new at this job and have a lot to catch up on, I've assigned Gabriella to bring you up to speed on the Landisil-IntimiRose venture. Gabriella, you'll be reporting to Jason in the meantime."

"What?" Gabriella cried out. Her face paled.

She turned and gave him a look so cold he could have frozen over.

Jason knew from that moment that he was in trouble.

CHAPTER 6

"This is insane, David. Are you really my brother?" Gabriella said. Her brother had gone nuts.

"It's only for a short time," David responded. "I figured the transition would be easier for him if the employees saw you were on board."

"I don't care how short it is. Why do I have to report to *him*? Isn't it already bad enough that I have to compete against him for the CEO position?" Gabriella saw Jason freeze at her words. "*He* didn't know?"

"Well, I planned to tell him today."

"David!"

"Sorry, sis. I made a mess of things, didn't I?"

"You sure did. How do you think it would look to the board?"

"Honestly, I assumed you weren't really interested in the spot."

"But you assumed wrong." Gabriella ran a hand over her hair. "I can't believe this."

"David, is it too late to reverse the decision?" Jason asked.

"I already sent the information across to HR," David muttered.

Crap. She was screwed, and worst of all, by her own brother. Gabriella didn't know whether to scream or pull her hair out.

"Is there anything we can do?" Jason asked.

"You've already done enough, thank you," Gabriella snapped. Then she felt a pang of guilt at her words. It wasn't his fault. But her day had just gone from ten to a hundred on a scale of how terrible it was.

A ringtone chimed, and David pulled out his phone. "Just a minute," he said as he glanced at the screen. Then he turned to Gabriella. "I need to leave immediately. I promised Mom I'd take Dad for his physical therapy appointment today. Could you show Jason to his office and bring him up to speed on the Landisil-IntimiRose venture? It's the newly renovated office on your floor. Thanks," he said as he patted her shoulder. "Jason, I'll catch up with you later."

"Sounds good," Jason said.

At least David had done one thing right and placed him on the same floor as her. She would have exploded all over him if he'd given Jason her father's office. But why couldn't he have just asked one of the executive assistants to take Jason to his office? Even Lacey would have been willing to do the job.

David didn't wait for her reply as he grabbed his jacket and strode out of the office, leaving her standing alone with Jason.

Suddenly, the room felt warmer than before. Gabriella was still in a daze about everything that had just happened, but she couldn't deny that being alone with Jason had heightened her awareness of him.

She brushed off the feeling. This wasn't time to allow her emotions to overwhelm the reality in front of her. Her brother had just made her fight for the CEO position much harder than it should be. The deed was done, and she had no choice but to live with it, but that didn't mean her brother was off the hook. She wasn't obligated to make it easy for Jason either.

Jason Silvers was now her enemy, and that overrode everything else including what her heart was trying to tell her. Gabriella was confident she'd win the CEO spot, despite what he brought to the table.

She took a deep breath and squared her shoulders. "Let's go," she said.

CHAPTER 7

Gabriella led the way out of David's office to the elevators. This set of private elevators only opened on the top three floors of the office building where the company's executives had offices. Gabriella entered the one that had arrived, punched in her floor button, and pressed her access card against the reader. She watched the doors close, and the elevator began its descent.

Jason stood beside her and said nothing. His woody mint-citrus scent wafted up her nostrils, and she resisted the urge to lean into it.

The elevator jolted, throwing her backwards, but strong arms caught her before she could crash into the back wall. "I've got you," Jason said.

His simple touch warmed and soothed her. Gabriella felt the tension in her body ease away, and she fought the desire to sink further into his arms and rest her head against his broad chest. But then his arms dropped, and she felt cold, bereft of his touch.

Get a grip, Gabriella, she said to herself. *He's your enemy and not a friend.*

She straightened and muttered a quick thanks. Fortunately, the elevators arrived on her floor at that moment, relieving her of the awkwardness she'd suddenly felt after what just happened.

Gabriella led the way till they arrived at Jason's new office. It was decorated in the same hues as David's office, though not as large. The desk in his outer office still remained empty, and Gabriella sent a quick text to Lacey to assign one of the executive assistants to his office.

Jason settled into the three-seater modern dark grey sofa in the space, while Gabriella took the adjacent two-seater. Her plan was to give him a quick overview of the venture and then get back to her office as soon as possible.

"Thanks for taking the time to bring me here," Jason said.

"No worries."

"Can I call you Gabriella, or would you prefer Ms. Landi?"

She thought for a moment. "You can call me Gabriella in private, but Dr. Landi before the staff."

"You have a PhD?"

"Yes, in materials engineering."

"Nice," he said with a smile. "You know, I had no idea you were David's sister when I met you that day. You've changed so much, and in a great way."

"Thank you." Her heart grew lighter at his compliment, but that didn't mean she wasn't going to keep him at arm's length. Besides, she didn't like a reminder of the day the blackmail started.

"I'm sorry that my presence here has made things difficult for you."

"It doesn't change anything," she said. "The CEO position is mine." Jason chuckled. "What's funny?"

"I love your confidence. But since David has also made the offer to me, I plan to give it my best shot, even though you have the home court advantage."

"We'll see about that. Can we talk about the joint venture?" She got up and pressed a button on the wall. A screen descended near the walls closest to where they sat.

Gabriella picked up a remote she'd spotted on the coffee table and pressed the ON button. A faint whirling sound filled the air as the projector came on and within a few minutes she had connected her phone to it wirelessly—all the projectors in the company were connected on the office IT network. She pulled up a presentation she'd used numerous times when speaking to buyers in preparation for the IntimiRose fashion show and began talking Jason through it.

How she managed to concentrate throughout the discussion was a mystery to her. She became keenly aware of Jason's every move, from the way his brow furrowed as he listened to her, to how his masculine hand rubbed his strong jaw line when he pondered something she'd said, to the way his broad shoulders relaxed against the sofa right before he asked a question.

Thirty minutes later, their discussion was

finished, and Gabriella disconnected her phone from the projector.

"That was a great overview," Jason said. "Thank you."

"You're welcome." She got up. It was time to leave.

"Can I ask for one more favor?" Jason asked.

"What is it?"

"I'd like to go and visit IntimiRose. Could you take me over there and introduce me to the CEO? David mentioned she would be open to a visit anytime."

Gabriella looked at her watch. She had a meeting coming up in the next fifteen minutes, and she couldn't afford to miss it. "I'm sorry," she said. "I have a business meeting to attend."

The phone on his desk rang at that moment.

Jason got up, headed over, and picked up the receiver. "Dr. Silvers speaking." He listened and then said, "Hold on," and extended the receiver to Gabriella. "It's for you."

Who could be calling her on his line? The only person that knew she was here was David.

She accepted the receiver and then placed the phone on speakerphone. "This is Dr. Landi."

"I just wanted to let you know your next

meeting has been postponed to tomorrow," Lacey's voice said loud and clear from the other end of the line.

Gabriella glanced at Jason. "Why?"

"Your brother rescheduled the meeting for Friday, saying he'd like to be present for it."

Was that really why David had pushed the meeting, or had he expected Jason would want to visit IntimiRose? Whatever the reason, her schedule was now open, and she had no excuse to deny Jason's request. "Thanks, Lacey. I'll be out of the office for the next few hours. Could you drop off the documents for the sales team as discussed? You can call me on my cell if you need me."

"I'll drop them off right now."

"Okay, talk to you later." Gabriella ended the call.

"Does that mean …?"

"Yes, I'll take you there. Let me send the CEO a quick text to let her know we're on our way."

"Are we going to take my car or yours?"

"Why don't we take our separate cars and meet there?"

"I still have some questions for you, and I'm

not sure whether I'll get the chance to grill you again anytime soon."

True, especially since she planned to go out of her way to avoid him. "Okay, let's take mine. I'll have to stop by my office and grab my purse and car keys. We'll meet in the parking garage near the reserved spots for executives. You do know where that is, right?"

"Yes. I'll see you there."

Jason rubbed his jaw. Why had he come up with the excuse that he had questions? This was so unlike him. Sure, he was curious about her, but that wasn't enough reason to have insisted on it when he didn't even have any questions in mind. Now Gabriella kept glancing at him, waiting for him to grill her as they drove toward the wealthier area of town. *Wait!* Why were they going this way instead of the downtown area where IntimiRose offices were located?

"I thought we were going to the IntimiRose headquarters," Jason said.

Gabriella shook her head. "It's best to meet

the CEO at her home where she prefers to work from."

"Okay. Can you tell me a little bit about her?"

"For one, she's David's mother-in-law, so you have to keep that in mind."

"David already mentioned that. How is she to work with?"

"She's very design-focused. That's how she's been able to make IntimiRose a force to be reckoned with in the lingerie industry. She's also passionate about anything related to breast cancer."

"Is this because of the family history of breast cancer?"

"Yes, but more especially for survivors like Jasmine, who had a preventative double mastectomy."

Jason had heard she'd had the surgery. They had to be truly in love to have loved each other through it—Jason knew most men would have taken to the hills.

"Oh, and if she had her way, we would all be in relationships," Gabriella continued.

"She's very direct about asking?"

"Absolutely," she responded with a chuckle.

"Oh boy."

"But she doesn't meddle if you're already in one. That shouldn't be a problem for you."

"Says who?"

Gabriella glanced sharply at him. "I thought you were engaged."

"Not anymore. She ended it a few weeks ago."

"I'm sorry."

"It's nothing." He didn't like talking about it. It reminded him too much about why she'd broken the engagement, leaving a bitter taste in his mouth. That part of his life was over, and there was no sense in reliving it. He turned and stared out the window, watching as the houses zoomed past.

But he had to know. "What about you?"

"What?"

"Are you in a relationship?"

A shadow fell over her face, and she stayed silent for a few minutes. Jason wondered what was going on in her mind. "No," she said finally.

Now why did his heart feel lighter just hearing that one word? *Get a grip on yourself, Jason.* A relationship wasn't right for him now.

He'd just gotten out of one, and he didn't need another. But he had to admit he was surprised. Gabriella was a beautiful young woman, though the cheerfulness and lightness he'd appreciated about her when they were young seemed to be missing. What had taken those away?

Gabriella seemed lost in her own world after that, and Jason didn't have the heart to intrude. They drove in silence for a few more minutes. Then Gabriella brought the car to a halt.

"We're here," she said.

Jason didn't know what he was expecting IntimiRose's CEO to look like, but certainly not the chic lady with glowing skin and dark hair done up in a loose chignon. She was dressed in a pink billowy blouse paired with black skinny jeans. Leah Banks looked more like Jasmine's sister than mother!

She pulled Jason into a hug as they stood in the foyer of the large home. "It's nice to finally meet you, Jason Silvers. David has spoken a lot about you. And my, you're a good looking one. Are you in a relationship?"

Jason heard a chuckle behind him, and his ears warmed. Well, this was certainly direct. But he had to admit Mrs. Banks was charming in her own way. She was a breath of fresh air, very different from his own mother. Audrey Silvers might have thought Leah Banks a bit too sentimental. He gave her a warm smile. "I'm not," he said.

"Perfect." She released him and turned to Gabriella. "Don't you think he'd make a great husband?"

Gabriella's chuckle turned into coughing, and Jason resisted the urge to laugh. He was sure she'd never expected the tables to turn on her, and he couldn't resist the opportunity to poke some fun at her.

"I'd love to be her husband, Mrs. Banks, but I think she's going to turn me down." Jason watched Gabriella's face turn a crimson red. She looked like she'd choke him if she could.

"Why on earth?" Mrs. Banks looked from Jason to Gabriella.

"She's been shooting daggers at me all morning, which hurts since we're old friends. I'd love to take her out for dinner and catch up on old times. I remember a certain young girl who—"

"Stop!" Gabriella cried out and grabbed his arm. The touch sent unexpected sparks of electricity through him.

Jason's heart beat faster. What was it about Gabriella that made him react in this strange way?

"Gabriella?" Mrs. Banks had a curious look on her face as she stared at them.

"Yes, Aunt Leah?"

"A dinner with him wouldn't hurt, right?"

"But—"

"Let me finish. You work too hard. Sometimes, it's okay to let your hair down. You're young, and you still have your whole life ahead of you, more than enough time to run a company. Yes, I know about your dream," she said at Gabriella's shocked look. "One night of dinner with him might do you good. Promise me you'll try. How about this weekend?"

Gabriella shot him a dark look, but Jason kept his face serene. He couldn't afford to mess things up. Somehow, the thought of dinner with Gabriella really appealed to him.

"Okay," Gabriella finally responded.

Mrs. Banks nodded in appreciation. "Fantastic. And you, young man, I expect you to be on your best behavior."

"Yes, ma'am," Jason responded. Gabriella was still holding onto his arm, and he was enjoying every minute of it.

She must have realized what she was doing because she dropped his arm like a hot potato. Jason felt a keen loss at the absence of her touch.

"Okay, why don't we go in and have a good chat about IntimiRose?" Mrs. Banks said and led the way into the rest of the home.

"Thank you for your time and for the meal," Jason said to Mrs. Banks as they stood in the living room. The conversation had been very insightful and entertaining. Mrs. Banks had managed to discuss business while keeping them in stitches the whole time. Now he could see why David raved about his mother-in-law. But more than that, it had been wonderful to see Gabriella so relaxed. He'd had a hard time keeping his eyes off her the whole time.

"Thank you, Aunt Leah," Gabriella chimed in.

"My pleasure," Mrs. Banks responded with a smile.

A door opened, and Jason turned to see a tall gentleman with salt and pepper hair dressed in a spring jacket and jeans walk in through a pair of French doors off the side of the living room. Jason could see the doors led to a garden, and the man held a pair of work gloves in his hands.

The man walked over to Mrs. Banks and gave her a big kiss on the lips. Jason watched, amused, as Mrs. Banks turned red and then gave him a playful pat on the chest.

This was most likely Mr. Banks, Jasmine's father. It was interesting to see such open genuine displays of affection between a couple that had been married for a long time. His parents' relationship was nothing like this, and Jason sometimes wondered if they even cared for each other. This was the type of marriage he would have loved if he ever got married, but it was also the kind that people of his background never got a chance to experience. It would really be a miracle if it happened to him.

The man then turned to them. "Hello," he said with a smile.

"This is my husband, Edward," Mrs. Banks

said. "Honey, you know Gabriella, and this is Jason, Gabriella's husband-to-be. Don't they look great together?"

"They sure do," Mr. Banks responded.

Jason laughed as he stood to his feet. It seemed Mrs. Banks was really serious about getting them together, an idea he didn't seem to mind, though a relationship was far from his mind at this time. "Nice to meet you, Mr. Banks."

"Welcome to the family, young man," Mr. Banks said as he extended his hand for a shake. Jason shook it—his grip was firm just like he'd expected.

"He's just a friend," Gabriella protested from beside him. Well, that was an improvement. She'd been giving off vibes like she considered him an enemy.

"That's what they all say in the beginning," Mr. Banks countered. Gabriella groaned, and Jason couldn't resist a chuckle. "But I'm watching you, young man. You have to treat her like the treasure she is."

"I will, sir." By now, Gabriella was practically foaming at the mouth. It was time to leave before she exploded. "It was great meeting you,

Mr. and Mrs. Banks."

"Same here," Mrs. Banks replied. "Let me walk you to the door."

"It's not a problem, ma'am. We can find our way out."

Mrs. Banks waved away his concern. "Oh, please." She got up and led them to the foyer where they grabbed their jackets before stepping out of the house. The clear spring air had a bite to it, and Jason pulled his jacket closer.

"Jason, feel free to come over anytime you like," Mrs. Banks said. "You're always welcome here."

"I'll take you up on that, Mrs. Banks."

"Oh, please, call me Leah." She pulled him into a hug. "Don't be afraid to chase her," she whispered to him. "I could see you had your eyes on her the whole time."

Jason's face grew warm. How had she known? "I will," he replied.

"Great." She patted him on the back and then let go. "I'll see you guys some other time. Have a good trip back."

"We will," Jason said. By now, Gabriella had unlocked the car with the fob. He walked over to the driver's side and opened the door for her.

Gabriella strode to where he stood. "What are you doing?"

"Opening the door for you."

"Why? I'm driving."

"No one ever said you can't open the door for the driver. Why don't you enter? Mrs. Banks is still waiting."

Gabriella glanced at Mrs. Banks who gave her a cheery wave, which she returned. She entered the car, and Jason shut the door after her. Then he walked around the car and entered from the passenger side.

Mrs. Banks gave them a final wave and turned back into the house.

Gabriella started the car, and then they were on their way.

"Thanks for bringing me here," Jason said.

"Where would you like me to drop you off?"

Ouch. He'd thought she would be more open to converse after the wonderful time they'd had at the Banks' house, but it seemed she was back to her prickly self.

"At home is fine."

She gave him a curious glance. "You're going home at *this* time?"

"My work day begins tomorrow. David was

going to be busy so he suggested I come in briefly today."

"Oh."

So she'd thought he was a slacker. How was that even possible for a breast surgeon? His thoughts soured. Or should he say former surgeon? A sharp pain sliced through his heart, and he gasped.

"Are you okay?" Gabriella asked.

He managed a small smile. "I'm fine." No matter what most people said, Jason didn't think he'd ever get over the devastation of losing his career.

She nodded and turned her eyes back on the road. "So where do you live?"

"On Bakers Street."

She gave him an incredulous look. "The one near my house?"

"Yes."

"Why?"

"What do you mean why?"

"I mean, there are lots of places you could have moved to, with much better houses. So why Bakers?"

"Because I like it. Eyes on the road, please."

Gabriella turned her eyes back on the traffic in front of her. "But it doesn't make sense."

"Why?"

"You're stinking rich. You can afford to buy all the houses on that street. I'm sure your parents won't be pleased you're staying there."

"It's what I like, and this place suits me just fine." Of course, there was no way he was going to tell her that he'd taken up the place because he'd wanted to be close to David's family. In addition, he wasn't interested in buying yet, and the place gave him the privacy and anonymity he wanted. None of his neighbors cared he was the sole heir to the Silvers empire.

Soon they arrived in front of the townhouse Jason lived in. "Thanks for the ride," he said. He'd stop by the office later in the evening to pick his car up.

She grunted in reply, but her mind seemed to be elsewhere.

Jason got out and shut the door behind him. He wondered what Gabriella was so preoccupied with as he walked up his front stairs and entered his home.

CHAPTER 9

Gabriella watched Jason go. For some reason, she was still angry at him for stepping back into her life and standing in the way of her chance at the top job. But most especially, she was mad at her brother for making it happen. She didn't typically get this worked up, and she needed to talk to someone about it. Also, the anxiety she seemed to have developed from the blackmail made everything worse. Unfortunately, she couldn't talk to anyone about *that*.

She picked up her phone and dialed a number. "Hi, Jasmine," she said.

"Hey, Gabriella," Jasmine said from the other end of the line.

"Is this a good time?"

"It's fine. What's up?"

"Not much."

"You sound tired. Is something wrong? What is it?"

Gabriella felt bad talking about it, but she was afraid the anger would eat her up from the inside if she didn't vent. Besides, Jasmine was also her childhood friend. "It's David."

"This doesn't sound good. You know what? I'm at David's place. Why don't you come over?"

"Are you sure? I don't want to disturb anything."

"Don't worry. Talking to you is now an emergency. Besides, he's not here, though he should be back soon after dropping off your dad. We have some time to ourselves."

"Okay, I'll be right there."

"See you soon."

~

Gabriella stepped out of the elevator into the large marble-tiled foyer that was the entrance to David's apartment. She strode through it, the glass door in front of her sliding open as she entered his living room.

The place was furnished in browns and blues, but Gabriella could see touches of red interspersed in the space that hadn't been there before. Probably from Jasmine. *Nice.*

The lady in question rushed forward and pulled her into a hug. "Hey, you," she said, giving Gabriella a once-over with her sparkling green eyes.

Gabriella leaned into the hug. Trust Jasmine to know she needed one. David was extremely lucky to have met such a wonderful person like Jasmine, though they'd butted heads from the beginning when their parents had pushed them together into an arranged marriage date. But there had been history between them, and their parents had figured it was time they faced the love they shared. Gabriella was glad it had worked out. It was the kind of love she wished she had a chance to experience. But 'failure at relationships' had become a byword for her, no matter how much she'd tried to make things work with each boyfriend. She let out a sigh.

"What's wrong?" Jasmine asked with worried eyes.

"Everything."

"Okay, let's sit down and talk about it." She led Gabriella to the sofa. "Do you want anything?"

Gabriella shook her head. "I just had lunch at your parents' place."

"For work?"

"Yes. Jason wanted to meet your mom and discuss the venture."

"David mentioned something about him joining the company. You know him? You called him by his first name."

"Yes, I first met him when I was a kid. But what makes me so mad is that David didn't even tell me about it beforehand, and then he offered the CEO candidacy to him!"

"Okay, that's a problem. Isn't that the spot you've been gunning for?"

"Right? Why do you get it when David doesn't seem to? And you don't even work at the company."

"Guys can be so dumb sometimes. I'm sorry. That must really hurt."

Gabriella's chest tightened, and she fought back the tears that burned at the back of her eyelids. "It does. Is it because I'm a woman?

Does David think I'm not capable enough to lead his company? I've been there from the beginning, Jasmine, and I've worked just as hard to help the company grow to what it is today. I'm not saying I should automatically have the spot, but I should be given a fair chance. And David is my brother for goodness sake."

"That's probably why it hurts more. You feel betrayed."

"Yes, I do."

Jasmine hugged her and then rubbed her back. "I'm sorry. He's going to hear an earful from me when he gets back."

Gabriella felt the tension ease from her shoulders. "Thank you. For listening."

"You're welcome. That's what sisters are for." Jasmine released her. "So, you know Jason Silvers."

"Hmmm." She could feel her face heating up. Why was she feeling all tingly inside at the mere mention of his name?

Jasmine peered closer at her face. "Gabriella, you're blushing."

She coughed and turned her face away. "I'm not."

"Yes you are. I'm sensing a story here."

"It's nothing. We were just regular kids at the time."

"Why do I get the feeling that you might have had a crush on him? Though that would be understandable given how gorgeous he is."

"Jasmine!"

"Oh please, I love your brother, but my eyes are not dead. So, do you like him?"

"He's my enemy now."

"Enemies can become lovers. Your brother and I are a prime example."

"Your love was mutual."

"See?" Jasmine said with a knowing smile. "I knew you had a crush on him."

"Had is the operative word here. I don't even know the kind of person he is now."

"He's a breast surgeon. He just moved from Connecticut and started working at Dexington Medical. He seems nice."

No wonder she hadn't met him yet. She'd been busy with the fashion show and hadn't had time for anything else, even visiting her brother. And it seemed Jason had made his long-time dream come true. Even when she'd known him years ago, he'd been going on and on about becoming a surgeon. *Wait!* She looked at

Jasmine in confusion. "Why is he working at Landisil Silicone?"

"Something happened recently, though David won't tell me what. He says it's Jason's secret to say."

What could have made him drop his passion? He must be pretty upset about it.

Gabriella caught herself. What was she thinking? He was her enemy now, and that was all she should concern herself with. She noticed Jasmine staring at her. "What?"

"You like him."

"Wait. No."

"I remember he asked after you when he came to visit David. Maybe he likes you too."

Gabriella scoffed. "I don't think so. I was a kid when I knew him."

"Was he nice to you then?"

"Well—"

"So he was. Something about you must have stood out to him. From the few comments he made about you, it seems he enjoyed your company. And now you've grown into a beautiful woman. Nothing says he won't like you even more now."

"I doubt that's going to happen. Do you

know he's one of those old money people? I'm sure his parents are waiting in the wings with a fiancée for him, even though he says he's not in a relationship."

"You've already found out he isn't in one?" Jasmine gave a small laugh. "Yet you keep insisting you're not interested in him."

"I'm not! He's the one that asked first."

"See? He's interested."

Gabriella threw up her arms. "Oh, I can't win an argument with you."

Jasmine placed her hands on Gabriella's shoulders. "Relax, girlfriend. I'm just teasing. But don't shut the door on him. Maybe he's really the one for you."

Only if he resigned and left Landisil Silicone would she consider it for a minute. Otherwise, he was going to remain in the enemy zone. She couldn't afford to trip up and lose the one chance she'd worked hard and prepared for over the years. But it was time to change the topic.

"How's the wedding planning coming along?" Gabriella asked.

"Thank goodness my aunt Becca is coming

back into town. She'll be planning my wedding."

"That's wonderful!"

"I know. It's heaven-sent. Right now, my primary focus is on healing completely from the surgery, enjoying my relationship with David, and working hard on finishing my ObGyn residency. That's already a lot on my plate. I'm more than happy to hand off the planning to someone I trust. David has been doing his bit as well. I don't mind remaining in this apartment, but he's found a house he'd like me to consider."

"I can understand why. He bought this place when Heather was still alive. He wants to start with you in a new place. New beginnings."

"I guessed as much. That's why I didn't push back on it. He seems to like the new house, and we'll be going there this weekend to look at it. Why don't you come along? It would be more fun with you around."

It would be hilarious. Jasmine and Gabriella did a pretty good job of ganging up on David whenever all three were together. She knew David secretly liked it, though he always protested to the contrary. But three would be a crowd, and she had no desire to be the third wheel. "I have an alumni event this weekend." One she hadn't planned on attending but was a good excuse to use.

"It would have been so much fun, but no worries." Gabriella heard the chime of the elevators. "That must be David."

Jasmine got up and strode to the glass door, her hands on her hips as she waited for David to enter.

"Hello, darling," David said as he came through and leaned forward to give her a kiss.

"Stop," Jasmine commanded with one hand in front of her. Gabriella fought a smile as she watched David halt in mid-air. "I'm mad at you."

David's hands dropped to his sides. "What is it, babe?"

"How could you treat Gabriella this way?"

Gabriella chuckled as she watched Jasmine grill David. Was this still the David she knew? She'd never seen her brother so compliant as he listened and then tried to explain himself.

David shot a pleading look at Gabriella, but she only shrugged her shoulders. He had to dig himself out of this one.

"I'm sorry, babe. It wasn't my intention."

"But you hurt her. Even I knew she wanted the CEO position. How could her own brother not know?"

"She looked tired all the time, and I was worried about her. I thought it might help."

"He even made me report to Jason," Gabriella chimed in.

Jasmine gave David an incredulous stare. "What?"

Gabriella held back a grin as David practically wilted. "Babe, I'm sorry," he said.

"I'm not the one you should be apologizing to." Jasmine let out a sigh. "You made a real mess this time, David. We women already have a tough time proving ourselves in the workplace, and you made it worse for Gabriella. You promised to protect her as her big brother."

David turned to Gabriella. "I'm sorry, Ella. I was wrong."

Gabriella could feel the sincerity in his apology. She'd known all along her brother hadn't meant to make things hard for her, but it had hurt all the same. "Okay."

"Now you can give me that kiss you owe me," Jasmine said with a smile.

David grabbed her in a hug and gave

Jasmine a kiss that even had Gabriella blushing. Even though he was her brother, this was too much PDA for her. Time to leave the lovebirds. "I'm heading out," she called out as she moved toward the exit.

"You're not staying?" David said as he disengaged from Jasmine. "I just got here."

"Guys, I need to keep my eyes pure."

She left amid the laughter that followed and entered the elevator that took her to the parking garage.

Gabriella got into her car and leaned back against the headrest. She was glad she'd come—it was like a weight had been rolled off her shoulders.

But now she had to face the music of working everyday with Jason alone.

CHAPTER 10

A few days later, Gabriella sat in her office reviewing the company's quarterly sales financials. So far, the company had exceeded its sales projections for the last two months and was on track to do so again this month.

She smiled to herself. She loved seeing the numbers that showed how hard she and her team had worked. She could only imagine how much better the numbers would look once the SK101 project was finished.

Her phone rang, and she picked up the call without looking at the screen. "This is Dr. Landi."

"I want you to send fifty thousand dollars to the account number," a distorted voice said.

Gabriella froze, and her heart raced. It was the blackmailer. She'd assumed he'd gone away when she hadn't heard from him for a while—clearly her own delusion. But fifty thousand dollars? That was highway robbery! "I don't have that kind of money."

"We both know you do. Don't push your luck. Send that money within twenty-four hours or …." The line went dead.

He didn't have to finish the statement. She knew exactly what he meant. *No, please.* She couldn't let that happen. The thought of her pictures all over the internet for everyone to see was enough to send her into a panic.

Breathe, Gabriella, breathe. Gabriella searched for the paper bag she kept hidden in her desk drawer, held it over her nose and mouth, and took steady breaths till she felt herself calm down. She slumped against her chair as her breathing return to normal.

How long could she continue like this? It wasn't only about the money—she had enough to last her a lifetime. But the blackmail was like a parasite, sucking her dry and eating into her one bite at a time. Gabriella feared it wasn't long before she became a shadow of her confident self. What had she done wrong to deserve all this?

She needed a plan, but what? She'd spent countless nights thinking about a solution, but she'd come up with nothing so far. *Please, God, help me*, she prayed. Her life was disintegrating bit by bit, and there was nothing she could do to stop it.

Her phone pinged, and she started. She picked it up and saw it was a calendar reminder about her upcoming meeting.

She laid the phone back on her desk. She couldn't let the blackmail take over her life.

For now, she had a meeting to attend, and a CEO job she needed to win.

For now, she had to pretend that everything was alright.

Gabriella found the office buzzing when she came down to the floor where the sales and marketing team resided. Employees were clustered in groups around the cubicles when she walked in, but they dispersed as soon as they saw her.

She soon reached the Director of Sales' office. Sam was her direct report and her trusted right hand man who managed the twenty-man sales team. Her brother had poached him from another startup, and it'd been one of the best decisions he'd made for the company. Sam had proven his worth multiple times over. The unassuming man was typing furiously away on his computer when she entered.

He looked up and gave her a broad smile. "Dr. Landi."

"Hello, Sam. Busy day?"

"Just the way I like it."

"What's going on out there?" Gabriella gestured at the main area outside his office. Sam was someone who had his ears to the ground, even though he kept his head down on his work.

"Someone posted a picture of Sandra Marks on the intranet, probably sometime last night." At Gabriella's questioning look, he said, "She was skunk drunk and looked awful."

Gabriella stiffened. Though Sandra wasn't

particularly liked in the office, posting such a picture where everyone in the company could see was embarrassing and mean-spirited. She'd been exposed in a particularly vulnerable state and had become the talk of the company, and not for the right reasons. No one deserved that no matter how terrible he or she was, and the company had zero tolerance for bullying of any kind. "Is it still up?" she asked.

"Yes," Sam confirmed.

She jumped to her feet. "Sam, call IT and get them to pull down that picture. Tell them I want the name of the employee who put up that photo in the next six hours. Otherwise, they should consider looking for another job."

"On it," Sam responded.

Gabriella strode out of Sam's office to the main area. "Can I get everyone's attention?" she said. All eyes turned to her. "It's time to focus on work. Anyone caught discussing the picture on the intranet will get a visit from HR."

Murmurs filled the area as the employees whispered to each other.

"Since it appears you guys aren't busy enough, please note that the sales target for the next quarter has been increased by ten percent."

The murmurs grew to groans. "It's not fair!" someone cried out.

Others muttered their agreement.

"It doesn't matter," Gabriella countered. "You became complicit to it by turning a blind eye. I heard the picture has been up for a couple of hours. Anyone of you could have reported it to management."

There were more groans.

Gabriella felt a hand on her arm. She turned to see Jason standing next to her wearing a three-piece suit without the jacket. Her heart rate increased. *Traitor*, she told herself. *Can't you even pretend not to be affected by him?*

"Can I see you for a moment?" Jason asked quietly.

"I'm not done yet," Gabriella countered.

"Now, please," he said while keeping a sweet smile on his face.

"Everyone, get back to work," she said and then left the main area with her head held high and headed toward the elevators. She could hear his footsteps as he followed behind her.

She was about to press the elevator button, when Jason grabbed her arm and steered her toward a conference room a few feet away.

"Let me go!" she said.

Jason held onto her arm till they entered the conference room. It was empty, and he shut the door behind her.

Then he turned to her, fury written all over his face. "What was that all about?"

"What are you talking about?" Gabriella countered.

"I heard you threatened to fire the IT folks if they didn't find the perp."

"At least we agree that someone did something terrible."

"But threaten their jobs? Do you want a lawsuit on your hands?"

"This is a serious situation, and I don't want to see a precedent in the company that anyone can put up whatever they like on the intranet and get away with it. It's part of IT's job description to safeguard the security of the company's intranet. Why won't they get fired if they don't do their jobs?"

"You can catch more flies with honey."

"I'm not here to make friends. I'm here to do my job."

"And why did you penalize the sales and marketing team back there? It's human nature to gossip, and you could have made your point without it."

So now he was the one schooling her? "We're going to have to agree to disagree."

Jason ran a hand through his hair. "I'm not going to tell you how to run your team, but doing this does not exactly endear you to the staff. You have to admit you went overboard there. What's going on?"

Okay, maybe she was a *little* extra pissed because of the blackmail issue. Why did he think she was his personal ATM? But it was none of Jason's business. "Nothing. By the way, how did you hear about it?"

"Sam called me."

That traitor. So he'd already gone over to Jason's side, even though it was just Jason's first week at work. "Anyway, I can't see what I did wrong. Our methods of leadership are just different. I'd prefer if you stay out of my business."

"Gabriella—"

Goodness. Her body was planning to kill her with the way her heart flipped at the mention of her name on his lips. "I'm Dr. Landi."

“You said I could call you Gabriella in private.”

“But we’re in the office. I meant private as in outside the office.”

He took a step closer to her. “So you’d like to see me outside the office.”

Gabriella’s cheeks warmed as she froze. *No no no.* She wasn’t ready to go there. Couldn’t he just stay on topic?

“I remember a certain person agreed to dinner with me over the weekend,” he said.

She’d thought he would forget. There was no way she was eating out with him. All her guards against him needed to stay firmly in place. “I have an alumni event to attend this weekend,” she murmured.

His face fell. “Really? Okay, it can’t be helped. But you owe me.”

Gabriella let loose the breath she’d been holding and headed toward the door. She had to keep Jason at arm’s length no matter what. “Owe you? I wasn’t the person who brought up the dinner.” She swung the conference door open and looked back. “Just stay out of my business,” she said and slammed the door behind her.

She hadn't planned to attend the alumni weekend, but now she was going to go just to keep her word.

CHAPTER 11

Gabriella got out of the car and straightened the purple dress she was wearing. She loved her blouses and slacks, but weekends were the only time she ever wore dresses of any sort. She'd gone shopping yesterday, and it had been love at first sight when she'd seen this dress. It was high-necked but accentuated her narrow waist before flowing out all the way to her ankles. She'd donned a grey military-style jacket over it and paired it with four-inch Jimmy Choo high heels. She was ready for war.

Gabriella was one hundred percent certain she was going to run into her ex-boyfriend. She'd met Scott at a previous alumni program, and they'd hit it off then. Gabriella had believed at the time he was the one. But when she'd found out he was cheating on her and she'd called off the relationship, she'd seen an ugly side of him. And that wasn't even mentioning the gambling she'd heard about later. Since then, Gabriella had kept away from any event he might attend. Knowing him, he might go out of his way to embarrass her. But she didn't see any point in avoiding him forever—she'd done nothing wrong.

She strode into the restaurant and requested the private room where the get-together was taking place. A waiter led her to the room and then left her. Gabriella took a deep breath, exhaled, and entered the room.

Over thirty pairs of eyes turned to her as she scanned the room for any empty seat around the large table. Her heart sank as she noticed her ex-boyfriend, Scott, sitting at the far right corner with a lady—dressed in a *little* black dress that exposed more than it hid—clinging to his arm. Scott shot her an angry look, but Gabriella ignored him and instead focused on the empty seat she'd spotted.

She called out her greetings as she went

along and made her way to the empty chair. Gabriella sank into it gratefully and motioned to one of the waiters that stood at the far corner. He came over and took her drink order. By now, everyone had turned back to their discussions.

"Hello, Gabriella," a voice said from beside her. Gabriella turned to see one of her good friends, Caitlin, sitting next to her.

"I didn't know you were here," Gabriella said as she gave her a warm smile.

"I had no idea I'd be here either, but my mother-in-law took the kids for the weekend, and my husband is out of town on a business trip. So I figured why not?"

"Good for you." Caitlin had gotten married to her high school sweetheart in college and already had three kids.

"But I already miss those naughty munchkins. I thought you weren't coming."

"I wasn't, but I changed my mind at the last minute."

"I'm glad you came."

"Me too. So what's going on?"

"Just general chit-chat. You know how everyone likes to toot their own horn."

Gabriella gave a small smile. Yes, it was nice

to see everyone and catch up with what was going on in their lives, but quite a number also used it as an opportunity both to show off any successes they'd had and make deals. It wasn't really Gabriella's thing, which was why she only attended such gatherings occasionally.

Gabriella spent the next few minutes chatting and catching up with her classmates. She managed to hear about a client that was looking for a silicone-based product, and Gabriella promised to follow up later with the lead. By the time she looked at her watch, more than an hour had passed, and it was time to start heading home.

She bade Caitlin farewell and got up to leave.

"Gabriella Landi," a voice said from across the table. It was Scott, the creep she didn't want anything to do with. The room fell silent at his voice. It was as if they were waiting for a showdown of some sort.

Gabriella forced a blank expression on her face. "Scott."

"I'm surprised to see you here."

"Why wouldn't I be here? I didn't know there was a law against my coming here."

Scott picked at his fingers with a knife. The

clingy lady was nowhere to be seen. "I thought you wouldn't show your face, considering the pictures."

Gabriella's mind whirled. What pictures? The only pictures she was afraid of … She took a sharp inhale. Was Scott the blackmailer?

The grin on his face said it all. In that moment, the memories she'd chosen to forget came rushing back.

Scott had invited her to Cape Cod for the weekend. Gabriella's family had a house there, so she'd opted to spend the night in it instead of at his parents' place. A few hours later, Gabriella had received an anonymous picture of Scott kissing another woman. He'd been wearing the same clothes she'd seen him in earlier that day. She'd headed out the next day to the restaurant they'd planned to meet up at and had called off the relationship.

Scott had blown his top in the private room they were in and called her all sorts of names before storming out of the restaurant. And he hadn't denied kissing the other woman. Gabriella had watched him leave, relieved she'd found out the kind of person he truly was.

She'd left briefly to use the bathroom and

then came back and ate the meal she'd already ordered. But that was the last thing she remembered before she woke up a few hours later in the restaurant when a waitress had nudged her awake. Gabriella had no idea what had happened in the hours prior, and an interview of the staff had revealed nothing. A quick visit to the hospital had shown she hadn't been raped and had no drugs in her system, so she'd decided to put the whole incident behind her.

Until the anonymous call had come, and the picture with it. She'd realized the photos might have been taken when she was unconscious at the restaurant, but she'd had no idea who the culprit was. She'd never imagined Scott could stoop so low. He must have spiked her drink in some way.

Gabriella trembled in anger. She didn't trust herself to speak without exploding. It was too late to report the incident, and fingering him as the blackmailer would only trigger him to release the pictures, the very thing she didn't want.

But how dare he blackmail her and then mention the photos here. She could hear her classmates whispering to each other, their minds running wild, wondering what pictures Scott was talking about. She was pretty sure a few of them would be willing to pay to get their hands on them.

But this was a mind game, one that Scott had no idea she was good at. There was no way he was ready to give up the pictures, since it would mean the money would dry up, funds he seemed to desperately need. But he'd made a mistake—now she knew the face of her enemy.

She squared her shoulders and looked him straight in the eye. "What pictures? If you have them, show us." Scott's jaw tightened. "I thought so. Now if you'll all excuse me, I have another appointment to make."

Gabriella walked away from her side of the table and made her way to the door. Just a few more steps and she could breathe easily again.

Someone bumped into her, and a glass of wine poured down the front of her dress. Gabriella heard the collective gasp but managed to keep her face blank as she watched dark streaks run down the dress all the way to its hem.

"I'm sorry," a voice said. Gabriella looked up to see Scott's lady staring at her with hate-filled eyes. She was definitely not sorry. Even though her mouth said otherwise, the incident had been deliberate.

Hundred more steps. Gabriella held her head high and exited the room without looking back. She wound her way through the rest of the restaurant, noting the curious glances and whispering till she exited the place.

Twenty more steps. Then she would be back in her car.

A hand grabbed her arm. Her head snapped up only to see it was Scott.

Her blood boiled, and she knocked his hand off. "Get your filthy hands off me or I'll report you for sexual harassment." She turned and continued walking in the direction of her car. Gabriella could hear his shallow breathing behind her, and fear gripped her heart. What if he tried something worse? It was obvious Scott was off his hinges. She knew the second he tried to grab her arm again.

"Don't you dare touch her," said a familiar voice. The same one that made the butterflies in her stomach flutter.

Gabriella whirled around to see Jason

striding toward her with a determined look on his face.

Her shoulders relaxed. She'd never been so glad to see him. Enemy or not, Jason was here to save her, and that was all that mattered in this moment.

"Who the hell are you?" Scott bellowed.

"That's the question I should be asking you," Jason said as he reached her side and put an arm around her back. Gabriella relaxed against his arm, and his woody mint-citrus scent filled her nostrils.

"What does it matter to you?" Scott asked.

"I don't take kindly to anyone harassing my fiancée."

Fiancée? She appreciated Jason's help, but this was taking it too far. She made to wriggle out of his arm, but he held fast.

"Stay still," he whispered.

"It's not over, Gabriella Landi. Don't forget the pictures," Scott said before turning and heading back to the restaurant.

Gabriella heard a *click,* like that of a camera's, but a quick look around revealed nothing. She watched Scott leave and then knocked off Jason's arm.

"Ouch! That hurts," he said as he rubbed the spot she'd hit. "What was that for?"

"I'm very grateful for your help, and I'm glad you showed up." Gabriella cocked her head. "But fiancée? Really?"

Jason grinned. "It worked, didn't it? And is that such a bad idea?"

"Jason Silvers, is everything alright upstairs?"

He chuckled. "Why? You want to make it right?" Then his face turned serious. "Something tells me that guy is up to no good. Is anything the matter?"

Gabriella could tell he was genuinely concerned about her, and she could feel her walls beginning to crack. *No!* She couldn't allow that. And there was no way she was telling him about the blackmail.

She turned from him and headed to where her car was parked. Jason followed. "Everything is fine," she muttered halfheartedly.

"Are you sure you can drive? Besides, I have a feeling that guy is still watching us. We need to keep up the act. Let me drive you home."

"What about your car?"

"I'll come back and pick it up."

What Jason said made sense. Tonight's ordeal had been a little too much for her, and she didn't trust herself not to be distracted on the way home. "Okay." She handed her car keys over to him.

Jason opened the door for her and waited till she got in before he made his way to the driver's side and stepped in.

Gabriella put on her seat belt, reclined the seat, and closed her eyes. The incident had shaken her, and all she wanted now was to go home.

Even if it meant being driven by her enemy.

Jason rolled the car to a stop in front of David's parents' house.

He glanced at Gabriella. She was fast asleep in the passenger seat beside him. She looked so serene and vulnerable he didn't have the heart to wake her up. Jason adjusted his car seat, leaned back to wait, and thought about what had happened earlier this evening.

He'd had dinner at the restaurant with an old college friend of his who also lived in Dexington. The dinner had been fun and relaxing until he'd seen Gabriella dash out of the restaurant. He'd known immediately that something was wrong.

Jason had said a quick apology and goodbye

to his friend and rushed after Gabriella. That was when he'd seen that creep harassing her. Jason wasn't a violent man, but he'd wanted to beat down that guy. How dare he attempt to touch Gabriella? He'd been surprised how extreme his emotions had been but had clamped down on it to deal with the situation.

He had no idea why he'd felt that way. All these emotions, good and bad, were new and seemed to be tied to Gabriella. What was it about her that made him want to protect her at all costs? Even her angry outbursts at him amused him, though he hid it to avoid infuriating her any further.

But what was that about pictures? The Gabriella he knew wouldn't have tolerated that man, yet she'd said nothing when he'd mentioned the photos. Was it something he was holding over her head? Something that David didn't even know about? If that was the case, then Gabriella needed his help. Creeps like that guy never gave up. He would talk to her about it when she woke up.

A lock of Gabriella's dark hair fell over her face, and Jason brushed it behind her ear. Her hair felt soft, silky, and luxuriant. Jason pulled back his hand to resist the urge to keep touching it.

Her eyes opened, and a warm look made a fleeting appearance on her face before disappearing into the blank expression she loved to put on around him.

"We're here," he said.

She sat up and readjusted her seat before brushing back her hair. "Thank you for the ride."

"My pleasure."

"How are you getting home?"

"My place is close by, remember? But I have to go back to the restaurant and pick up my car. I'll grab a cab from the next street."

"Okay."

It was now or never. "Gabriella, you know you can talk to me if something's wrong."

Gabriella stiffened. "Thanks, but no thanks. I'd rather you just forget what happened tonight."

"Gabriella—"

"I don't want to talk about it. Goodnight, Jason." She opened the car door and stepped out.

Jason did the same, locked the car, and came over to her side. He handed her the car keys.

She accepted them and then walked up the front stairs of her home. Jason watched her open the door and disappear inside.

Something dangerous was going on with Gabriella, and he had to find out what it was before it was too late.

Time to put his charm to good use.

Jason exited the cab he'd arrived in and entered the restaurant.

The maître d' approached him. "Good evening, sir. How may I help you?"

"I'm supposed to meet a friend here," Jason replied. "She's attending an alumni event at this restaurant."

"Do you have a name, sir?"

"Dr. Gabriella Landi." Jason hoped someone who knew her well would be curious about who Gabriella's visitor was.

"One minute, please. Would you like to wait at the bar?"

"Sure."

The maître d' led the way, and soon Jason sat at the bar nursing a glass of sparkling water. He turned and studied the place as he waited. The restaurant seemed to have two private rooms as far as he could tell from the foot traffic. One group seemed to be having some sort of senior citizen celebration, while young men and women who looked to be about Gabriella's age paraded in and out of the second room. Jason guessed the alumni event was taking place in the latter.

Soon the manager returned with a young woman in tow and then left.

"Hello," the woman said as she adjusted the sensible glasses sitting on the bridge of her nose. "Are you looking for Gabriella?"

"Yes. I was told she'd be here."

"And who might you be?"

"I'm Jason Silvers, a friend of her brother's. And you are ..."

"Caitlin Summers, Gabriella's classmate."

"Nice to meet you, Caitlin. What about Gabriella? Is she still here?" Jason knew exactly where Gabriella was, but it was better to pretend otherwise to elicit the information he wanted.

Caitlin studied him for a moment and

seemed satisfied with what she saw. "She's gone."

"Gone? I thought the alumni event wasn't supposed to be over by now."

"There was an incident. Look, I probably shouldn't tell you this, but seeing you're her brother's friend and all ..."

Jason gave her an encouraging smile. "You can tell me. What happened?"

"She had a run-in with her ex-boyfriend, Scott Sanders. I never liked that guy, and I still don't know what Gabriella saw in him. But he insinuated he had some compromising pictures of Gabriella. I have no idea how he got said pictures, but he seemed rather confident they exist."

The muscle in Jason's jaw tightened. The creep probably had those pictures. "Anything else?"

Caitlin shook her head. "But Gabriella held her own. I'm proud of how she handled it. But now I'm worried if she's okay." Someone called Caitlin's name from the threshold of the private room. "Listen, I have to go."

"No worries. Thanks for telling me."

"Please take good care of her, okay?"

"I will."

"Bye." She turned and hurried to the private room and soon disappeared inside.

Jason turned back to his drink. So, that was what happened. His intuition had been right about the creep. He needed to find out more about Scott Sanders.

Jason dropped a twenty-dollar bill on the bar and headed out of the restaurant. On his way out, he spied the maître d' and slipped him a hundred-dollar bill. The maître d' thanked him profusely and held the door open for him.

Jason exited the place and strode over to where he'd parked his car. He got in, pulled out his phone, and speed-dialed a number.

"Jason! To what do I owe this honor?" a boisterous voice answered.

"How are you doing, Quinn?" Quinn was Jason's investigator friend. They'd met in college and had stayed in touch ever since. Quinn had his own private investigation firm, and Jason kept a retainer there for whenever he needed his help.

"Great, just great. I'm sure you didn't call me just to chit-chat."

"I have a problem."

"Tell me," Quinn said, his voice all serious.

Jason told him what he'd heard about Scott Sanders, which wasn't really much. "I need to find out more about him. And anything connecting him to Gabriella Landi."

"Consider it done."

"When will I hear back from you?"

"In twenty-four hours. I don't think it'd be that difficult to track him down."

"Alright. I'll wait for your call. Thanks, man."

"You're welcome. I'll get on it now."

"Talk to you later." He ended the call.

Jason was confident Quinn would find everything he needed to know.

For now, it was time to head home and wait for Quinn's call.

Twenty-four hours couldn't come soon enough.

"Are you saying this is blackmail?" Jason asked as he leaned against his car's headrest. He'd been too antsy all day waiting for Quinn's call and had come into the office to get some work done. He'd finished and had just entered his car when the call came through.

"It seems like it," Quinn said. "This guy, Scott, has quite a racket all set up. He'd woo these rich young women, go out with them, and then blackmail them. Most of them are too embarrassed to report him. He must have something over their head, I'm guessing the pictures in question. So far, nothing has been released yet for any of the cases—his blackmail must have been effective. He dated Gabriella Landi a couple of months ago, and then they broke up per his modus operandi. I'm pretty certain he's blackmailing her too. But I haven't found the money trail yet. He probably has an offshore account somewhere."

"Okay, I'll make a few calls to help with that. Anything else?"

"I found out he goes twice a week to the casino. I'm guessing he's burning through the money there." So the guy had a gambling problem. "But I'm going to keep digging to see what else I can find."

"Thanks, Quinn. I'll send you the information you need once I get it."

"Sounds good. Talk to you later." The line went dead.

Jason dropped his phone into the center console and leaned back.

So the creep had been blackmailing Gabriella. She must have been so stressed dealing with it alone—she probably hadn't told David or her family about it.

Well, Jason was going to put a stop to it.

It was time to come up with a plan that would free her from Scott's clutches.

CHAPTER 13

Gabriella sat up in bed the next morning feeling refreshed. She hadn't tossed all night like she had since the blackmail began, which was surprising given that it hadn't ended yet. The only change was Jason.

He'd stepped in when she'd least expected, a breath of fresh air in a stifling room. Gabriella blamed herself for becoming a victim of blackmail. If only she hadn't gone to Cape Cod. If only she'd never dated Scott. She'd been a poor judge of character, and it had cost her.

Gabriella had allowed herself to be swept off her feet by his glib tongue, and now she was paying dearly for it. Literally. But Jason had helped her, and she'd felt no longer alone in a spiraling vortex. But when he tried to pull her out, she'd panicked instead and had been rude to him.

She bunched her hair in her hands. *Grrr!* Why did he have to be her competitor? It made everything so awkward and complicated. Still, she had to apologize. But speaking to him might break down her vulnerable walls and open the can of worms that needed to stay closed.

She thought for a moment. Maybe she could sketch him a picture. She'd never given him one, but he'd always complimented her skills the times he'd seen her work. It would be a great peace offering, and the sketching process also might take her mind off things. Yes, it was the perfect solution. She didn't even have to hand it to him personally—she could just drop it off.

Gabriella rushed out of bed and hurried over to the alcove where her drawing supplies rested.

It was time to get started on that apology.

Hopefully, it wouldn't come back to bite her in the face.

~

Gabriella had spent the rest of the weekend sketching, and she now had the product of her efforts under her arm as she got off the elevator on Monday morning and made her way to her office. She had an early morning meeting to kick off the SK101 project, which she would take care of before heading to Jason's office to look for him.

He was usually in by now—it seemed he was an early riser—but Gabriella expected Jason to be out for a meeting with his team after that. She'd rather drop off a note with the sketch than speak to him.

As Gabriella passed Foster's office, she noticed his door was ajar. She made to move past but stopped in her tracks when she overheard Jason's name.

Her curiosity piqued, Gabriella moved closer to hear what Foster was saying.

"That Silvers guy is not a threat," Foster said to whoever he was speaking to on the phone as he turned in his swivel chair. "He's just a two-bit has-been surgeon who doesn't know what he's doing." Foster gave a sardonic laugh. "Does he think this company is the operating room? He's a waste of space, I tell you."

Gabriella clenched her hands into fists. What right did Foster have to disparage Jason? Sure, Jason didn't know everything, but who would after being in a new position for such a short time? Still, he'd progressed more than she'd expected, and Gabriella had only heard good things about him from the employees she'd talked to and even from a few board members.

Gabriella pushed the door wide open and stepped in. Foster looked up in shock, and then his face settled into a frown. "What are you doing in my office? You have no right to step in here."

Gabriella stood and looked down on him. "And you have no right tearing Dr. Silvers down. Now, how would my father feel when he hears what you've just said?"

Foster's face lost its color for a moment, but then he recovered. "Nothing is going to happen because you won't tell him."

"Why do you think so?"

"Because you wouldn't want him to have another stroke, would you?"

Gabriella's fists tightened further. "That's assuming you're important enough to be a concern, which I doubt is the case."

"Gabriella Landi, you—"

"Dr. Landi to you."

"You're going to regret this!" he said wagging a finger at her. "Don't think the CEO position is a slam dunk for you. I've heard some things about you."

Gabriella froze. "How dare you?"

"Dr. Landi, can I see you for a moment?" a familiar voice said behind her.

Gabriella turned to see Jason standing by the door in yet another sharp suit. How did he always manage to look so good in anything he wore?

"Dr. Landi, a minute," he insisted.

Gabriella glared once more at Foster and followed Jason out of the office.

"Can you imagine that man?" Gabriella said once Jason had shut his office door behind her.

"You were out of line, Dr. Landi," Jason said in a serious tone.

Gabriella looked at Jason in confusion. "What?"

"That man is old enough to be your father, yet you spoke that way to him."

Unbelievable. She probably wasn't hearing correctly. "Are you serious right now?"

"Dr. Landi—"

"Just stop. I can't believe this." She had defended him to Foster, yet here he was reprimanding her like a subordinate, reminding her of the position David had put her in. "And this is for you." She dropped the wrapped sketch on the desk. "Have a good day, Dr. Silvers."

"I'm not done—"

"But I am. Enjoy the rest of your day."

Gabriella walked out of his office.

CHAPTER 14

*J*ason stared after Gabriella as she left his office. Had he made yet another mistake?

He'd arrived for work and had overheard the conversation between Gabriella and Foster on his way to his office. Jason had been afraid Gabriella might make a mistake that would cost her the chance at the CEO position—Foster had deep connections to the board and could use something she said against her. And it would all be because of him.

He'd wanted to caution her, but it seemed his intentions might have come out all wrong.

Jason looked down at the package on his

desk. There was a note attached. He picked it up and opened it.

Thanks for your help, the note read. *Hope you like it.*

Jason tore open the package's wrapping and pulled out the item inside. It was a sketch of Jason and David laughing with their arms around each other's shoulders. She'd sketched him wearing the same clothes he'd had on the first day in David's office. Gabriella had somehow captured the joy and peace he felt with David but had never expressed. The sketch was so real it was hard to believe that the scene had never taken place. Jason had always loved her drawings, and this was another masterpiece.

He slumped into his chair. She'd had it with her, which meant she'd planned to give it to him. What if the conversation he'd overheard hadn't been everything? He'd seen a glimpse of hurt cross her face before it disappeared. What if he'd wronged her?

God, help me. He wasn't used to all this, yet at the same time he couldn't help being drawn to her. It was like there was someone behind the blank mask she loved to put on that was hoping to be set free, a person he felt desperate to meet.

One he might have had a glimpse of when he'd found out about the blackmail.

Jason had checked, and no pictures had been released on the internet, but that could still happen sooner or later. He'd spend the rest of the weekend thinking about what to do. Scott had to be stopped.

He'd decided on a plan this morning. It had to be executed without Gabriella finding out, which was a tough feat to accomplish. To do so, he needed help, and he knew the right man for the job. The sooner they took care of it, the better.

He picked up his phone and made a call.

And prayed his plan wouldn't backfire.

CHAPTER 15

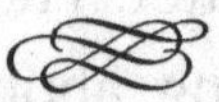

The doorbell chimed as Jason entered the coffee shop and looked around. The smell of fresh bread and coffee hung heavy in the air, while soft classical music played in the background. There were only a few customers in the place, which suited Jason just fine, though that could change pretty quickly once it was lunch hour.

Jason spotted David sitting in the back corner and studying what looked like a surgical journal.

His heart ached at the sight, reminding him too much of what he'd lost. There were days when he'd done the same, reading a journal on the latest surgical developments and sipping coffee at the same time. Would he ever hold a scalpel in the operating room again? Jason had started treatment, but he still had a long way to go. But he held out hope he'd have a chance again, despite what the doctors had said.

David looked up at that moment, and Jason gave him a small wave before making his way to where he was. He pulled out a chair and sat down once he reached the table.

David pushed the demitasse cup that was beside his mug across to Jason. "I took the liberty of ordering expresso for you."

"Thanks." Jason took a sip. It was hot, bitter, and rich, just the way he liked it.

"You said it was urgent," David said.

"It's about Gabriella."

David stilled. "What about her?"

Jason recounted what had happened the evening of the alumni event as well as what he'd found out so far. David's face grew darker and darker, and by the time Jason finished, he was afraid David might pop a vein.

"This is madness," David said as the muscle in his jaw line twitched.

"I couldn't believe it myself at first," Jason responded. "But we have to work quickly to stop the guy before he has a chance to reveal the pictures."

"Have you seen any of them?"

Jason shook his head. "I'm sure Gabriella received a copy—there's no way she'd pay the blackmail without it. I also took the liberty of making a few calls and found out she's been making regular payments to a bank account in the Cayman Islands. The same bank account that his other victims have paid into."

"Goodness. The guy is running a racket." David dropped his elbows on the table and leaned forward, a grim look on his face. "But he made the mistake of messing with my sister."

"Here's what I think we should do ..." Jason shared his plan with David.

David nodded his head once Jason had finished. "Yes, that would work. I'll get on my part right away. I know who to reach out to. They hate slimeballs like this guy."

"We just need to make sure Gabriella doesn't find out."

"I agree. It might hurt her pride that we intervened. There's one more thing left to do."

"What?"

"Let's pray about it."

The shrill ringtone pierced the air, and David snatched up his phone and answered it. He listened for a while and then responded, "Thanks, I owe you one," he said before ending the call.

"How did it go?" Jason asked. They were sitting in David's living room while they waited.

"Sanders fessed up. My guys managed to put the fear of God in him." David had told Jason that some of his ex-Army buddies, who had moved to the intelligence business, had picked Sanders up and taken him to an undisclosed location for interrogation. "They doubt he's going to make any more trouble in the near future. They plan to let him rest tonight, and then they'll drop him off tomorrow."

"I hope he wasn't too hurt."

David shook his head. "No, he sang before they really started. They'd already planned to go easy on him since they know my standards. The interrogation was more mental than anything else. They'd also spoken to your private investigator, and the information from Sanders on the location of the pictures matched the information he'd gathered." Quinn had reached out to a hacker friend who had followed Sanders' electronic footprint and found where he'd stashed the pictures. All the photos had been destroyed.

"But there's one thing that's bugging them," David said.

"What?"

"He had a look in his eyes that they've seen before. They think he might have withheld some information about the pictures, but they held off on pushing further because of my instructions. They also tried hard not to give away the fact that the photos they were really looking for were the ones related to Gabriella, so that might have hindered them too."

Jason thought quickly. "The information he might be withholding can't be about a photo stash."

"I agree. Since your guy's and Sanders' information are a match, I doubt that's the case."

"I wonder what it could be."

"At this point, we have to leave it in God's hands. We'll cross that bridge when we get to it."

The chime of the elevator to his penthouse filled the air. David and Jason looked at each other. "I wonder who it could be," David said as he got to his feet.

"Could it be Jasmine?"

David shook his head. "She's on-call tonight."

The glass door slid open, and Gabriella rushed in.

CHAPTER 16

Gabriella was still in shock over what had happened. She had to confirm if it was all true.

She called Jason's number, but it didn't go through. She tried her brother's line—it was busy. Gabriella got into her car and drove to the office, but Jason wasn't there either. She got back on the road, stopped by his place, and rang the bell for a few minutes. No one came to the door. Where could he be? Then she called Jasmine's number to see if she'd heard anything about either of them, and Jasmine suggested Jason might be at David's place.

Duh. Why hadn't she thought of that? She raced over to David's apartment and took his private elevator to the penthouse. Sure enough, the two men were there hanging out on the couch as she entered.

Gabriella could see from the looks on their faces she was the last person they'd expected to see. But it didn't matter. She had a purpose to achieve, and nothing or no one could stop her.

"Hello, sis," David said.

"Hi," she replied cheerily. She couldn't help the happiness that seeped into her voice. "Just the man I was looking for," she said and made a beeline for Jason.

A flash of confusion and panic crossed Jason's face. *He must be wondering what he'd done wrong this time.*

Gabriella felt a pang of conscience at his reaction. She'd given him a hard time, but it hadn't been intentional, and he'd sometimes deserved it. But his heart was in a good place, the magnitude of which she'd just found out.

How could she put into words what she was feeling right now? She'd thought she was trapped forever in the vortex of blackmail. She'd seen her anxiety grow with each call and had lost sleep and peace over it.

Now, she was free, finally and totally free!

And it was all because of this wonderful man lounging on the couch, dressed impeccably as always. He'd stepped in and shattered Scott's hold over her life. *Thank you, God.*

She reached where Jason sat, leaned forward and gave him a kiss on the cheek. "Thank you." Though they were only two words, Gabriella hoped he understood both were from the bottom of her heart and expressed how grateful she was to feel alive again. She pulled back and sat on the coffee table in front of him.

Jason froze, his face mirroring the shock and confusion that must be rippling through him. She had to explain. "My friend, Caitlin, just called and said someone had stopped by the evening of the alumni event to look for me, and she'd told him about the pictures. She didn't remember the name the man had given her, but her description fit you to a tee. It was you, right?"

Jason glanced at David, who nodded. He turned his eyes back on Gabriella. "Yes."

Gabriella clasped her hand over her mouth and stifled a cry. Getting the confirmation directly from him suddenly made it more real. It had really been him, pretending he was looking for her when all he'd probably wanted was information about the pictures! Then everything about the blackmail had ended only a few days later. It wasn't a coincidence.

"Hey, are you okay?" he asked softly.

She swallowed, took a deep breath, and then nodded. "After Caitlin's call, I got a text from Scott apologizing for the pictures and returning all the money I'd ever given him. He also mentioned the photos had been destroyed. And all this happened *after* you'd asked about the pictures. It was you, wasn't it, that made him stop?"

"It was us, your brother and I."

Gabriella stilled, overwhelmed by her emotions. He'd done it, this man who was supposed to be her enemy. Her walls cracked and collapsed, and a rush of love and appreciation flooded her heart. Words were no longer enough, and so she did the one thing she'd wanted to do since she'd met him again.

Gabriella leaned forward and hugged him tight. His woody mint-citrus scent washed over her, casting warm tendrils around her that made her burrow further into him. Her heart beat faster, and the butterflies in her stomach began to dance.

The room faded, and it was like they were the only two people around. She could hear the beats of his heart, and soon they synced with hers, each beat, music to her ears.

Gabriella let out a somewhat silent sigh of contentment. She'd tried so hard to deny it, but her heart had always known: this man was special, and he was the one her heart wanted.

Jason wrapped his arms around her, silently acknowledging he'd heard her. They fit perfectly into each other, and Gabriella wished she could just stay there forever.

Then David coughed, shattering the moment, and they broke apart.

"I'm so sorry," Gabriella said as her face warmed. "Thank you, Jason. And David." She gave her brother a wink, and then turned back to Jason. "How can I repay you?" she asked.

His next words were the last ones she expected to hear.

"Go out with me," he said.

~

Gabriella's eyes widened. Had Jason really said what she thought she'd heard? "What?"

"Go out with me, Gabriella," Jason repeated. "Be my girlfriend."

"Goodness, I wasn't expecting that one," David muttered. "Jason, we'll talk later." He picked up his keys and phone, donned his jacket, and left the apartment.

But Gabriella only had eyes for Jason. He'd really said it. She knew about the promise Jason had made to her brother many years ago to stay away from her. Now he'd broken that promise. It was a big deal.

She got up from the coffee table and settled on the couch beside him. "Are you just saying this in the heat of the moment? Because I can forget you ever asked if you like."

Jason maintained a steady gaze. "No. I really like you, Gabriella. I think I've liked you for a long time. I just didn't know it. Even if I had known, I wouldn't have been able to do anything about it at the time."

"Because of the engagement?"

"Yes. Even if it was an engagement I hated, I still had to be faithful to her."

Gabriella didn't know what to think. She was

still in shock. He was supposed to be her enemy, though her walls had already crumbled. A part of her yearned for the chance to explore a relationship with him, but she wasn't ready for love yet. She wasn't sure when she would be. She'd been hurt too many times, and her heart was covered in scabs. Also, her desire for the CEO position stood between them like a mountain. But she knew with every fiber of her being that she would regret it if she turned him down.

"So what do you say, Gabriella?" Jason asked.

"What about the CEO position?"

"We'll still fight for it as usual. I'm not expecting you to change that."

Gabriella let out a sigh of relief. She could live with that. "Yes."

Jason's eyes widened. "Seriously?"

"Yes. But you still have to deal with my brother."

"I know."

Then he pulled her into a hug, and Gabriella knew at that moment that she'd made the right decision.

CHAPTER 17

Jason stood as David returned to the apartment. He rubbed his sweaty palms on his jeans and swallowed. He'd seen Gabriella off, promising to call her back later tonight. They'd decided it was better for Jason to face David immediately, much like ripping off a bandaid at once, so Jason had remained behind to wait for him.

David shrugged off his coat. "What about Gabriella?" he asked.

"She's gone home."

David walked over and sat on the couch. "I guess we're having the talk."

"We sure are."

"What are you thinking, Jason?"

"That I really like your sister."

"Dude, we had an agreement."

"When she was little. But she's a full grown woman now if you haven't noticed."

"Come on, man."

"I'm sorry. I'm really sorry, David, but I like your sister. I think I always have, and in some subconscious way, you've always known."

"Jason, you're my best buddy, and I like you a lot. But we both know that though you guys haven't reached there yet, marriage is always in the picture, right?"

"Yes."

"Exactly. And as much as I love you, your mom is another story altogether."

Crap. He'd known it was going to come up. His mother was quite famous for her …. well, 'snobbery' was putting it lightly. Even though David was a self-made billionaire, and his family had a lot of money, it couldn't be compared with the old-money Silvers wealth, like his mother liked to remind him. It was already a given she was going to turn up her nose at Gabriella and kick against the relationship.

But Jason had made up his mind he was

going to fight hard. He'd fought once for his career and won, and he could win again and protect Gabriella at the same time. "David, I'm going to win over my mom while protecting Gabriella with my life. You've seen how I am when I'm passionate about something. I'm passionate about Gabriella, and I'm going to protect her with every fiber of my being."

David stared long and hard at Jason. There must have been some course in the Army that taught David how to stare this way.

Jason forced himself not to squirm.

"Okay," David finally said. "But if you break her heart, I'll break you."

Jason let out the breath he'd been holding. "Agreed."

"Alright, congratulations, man." He gave Jason a bro hug and then got up, grabbed two cans of soda from the refrigerator, and returned. He slid one across to Jason. "Oh, and one more thing?"

"What?"

"I don't want to hear about your lovey-dovey activities. That's just way too much for me."

Jason laughed. "Now you know how

Gabriella feels about your displays of affection with Jasmine."

"That's true," David said with a solemn nod. And then he broke into a grin. "Gabriella won't know what hit her with the ladies."

"You mean Alicia, Jasmine, and Dana?"

"Yes." David raised his can in a toast. "Welcome to the madness. Cheers."

Jason clinked his can with David's. "Cheers."

CHAPTER 18

Gabriella's phone rang as she lay on her bed. She was ready to sleep, but she'd promised Jason she'd wait for his call. "Hello," she said.

"Hey, beautiful," Jason's smooth voice said from the other end of the line, sending ripples through her.

Gabriella still found it hard to believe she was actually in a relationship with her one-time crush. She hadn't told her parents—it was early yet, and she was certain David would share the news faster than she ever would. They would find out eventually.

"How did it go?" she asked with a smile.

"It went great, all things considered. He didn't kill me, and that's a miracle."

Gabriella chuckled. "Don't worry, I would have brought you back to life if he did."

"Really? How?"

"Maybe with a kiss?"

"Why didn't you tell me before? I could have encouraged him to kill me."

Gabriella burst out laughing. It was fun to see this side of Jason. "That bad, huh?"

"Definitely."

"I'll keep that in mind."

"Thank you."

There was a moment of companionable silence. It was nice to hear the cadence of Jason's breathing from the other end of the line.

Gabriella broke the silence. "Tomorrow at the office is going to be awkward."

"Which would you prefer, hide it or let everyone find out?" Jason asked.

"Hmmm. Neither. Remain professional in the workplace, but sneak in a kiss or two whenever possible."

"Your mind is really on the kiss, isn't it?"

"Hey, I'm just trying to help you out here. We can forget the kisses if you like."

"Absolutely not. Your wish for kisses is my command."

Gabriella chuckled. "You're nuts."

"I'm nuts about you."

She laughed. "You're so cheesy." Gabriella changed positions and turned to her side.

"How are you feeling? Overwhelmed?" Jason asked.

"A little."

"We'll take it one day at a time, alright?"

"Okay." Gabriella stifled a yawn.

"Ah, it's time for your beauty sleep."

"I think so too."

"Goodnight, Gabriella. Sweet dreams."

"Goodnight, Jason." She ended the call.

Gabriella giggled as she tossed in bed. Dating Jason might just be more fun than she'd imagined.

Her phone rang again, and Gabriella picked up the call without looking at the screen. "Jason—"

"It's Jasmine, or more like Jasmine, Alicia, and Dana. We're on a conference call, and we've just added you in." Jasmine was a third-year ObGyn resident, Dana was a fourth-year general surgical resident, while Alicia was a third-year internal medicine resident. They were room-mates, and Gabriella envied their close friendship.

"Hello," Gabriella replied with a smile.

"Congratulations!" Alicia, Dana, and Jasmine said in unison.

Gabriella jerked in surprise. She hadn't expected *that*. "Thank you." News sure travelled fast.

"I told you he liked you," Jasmine said.

"I have to admit you were right."

"Welcome to the club," Dana said.

"Thank you," Gabriella responded.

"I know everyone is going to assume we'll smother you with wedding plans," Alicia said. "But we won't."

Gabriella was grateful for that. Marriage and babies were nowhere near her horizon. "How's Willow?"

"Being her ever bubbly self and giving the boys in her class a hard time. I feel like I've aged since she started school." Willow had been in the hospital for the longest time for cystic fibrosis and had finally gotten better after experimental treatments. She'd started school after that. "I imagine it would be worse if Blake wasn't there. His name seems to strike fear into the hearts of those little boys." Blake Dexington was Alicia's fiancé and the incoming CEO of Dexington Healthcare which owned Dexington Medical where Alicia, Jasmine, Dana, David, and even Jason, until recently, worked. The Dexingtons were considered the First Family of Dexington, the city that bore their name.

"I'm sure it'll get better," Gabriella said.

"I imagine it will, once we get married and move into the same house," Alicia replied. "Jasmine, I heard Aunt Becca is back." Jasmine's aunt, Rebecca Scott, was a socialite and planner extraordinaire for celeb weddings. She'd been out of the country for some time but had called to say she was returning soon.

"Hmmm. She got back last night with a surprise. I have a new niece."

"Really?" Alicia said.

"Yes, and the girl is cute too. Makes me want to have one of my own."

"I thought she wasn't married," Dana asked.

"She isn't," Jasmine responded. "But she hasn't said anything about the father, and we don't want to pressure her. She'll tell us whenever she's ready. We are just glad she's back home."

"I love children—they're so adorable," Dana said. "Sometimes, I wish I could have one of my own, but I'm grateful I have the option to adopt." Gabriella had heard Dana's story and how her womb had been destroyed in an accident, which had also killed her mom. But she'd found love with Josh Roman, a fellow surgeon who was more than happy to adopt.

"You should stop by sometime and come and play with Chloe."

"Oh, I'm definitely stopping by," Dana said. "Also, once Aunt Becca is all settled, we'll need to discuss my wedding plans. Gabriella, you should definitely join us for wedding shopping whenever you're free. We'd love to have you."

"Yes," Alicia and Jasmine echoed.

"Count me in," Gabriella said.

"Awesome," Dana responded.

"Okay, it's time to let the celebrant rest," Alicia said.

"Celebrant? We haven't even had cake," Jasmine said. "We need to throw a party."

Dana chuckled. "Ignore her, Gabriella.

Jasmine, I don't remember seeing any celebration before you locked lips with David."

"TMI, ladies, TMI," Gabriella said. "It's weird hearing such talks about my brother."

"Get used to it, honey," Jasmine said with a chuckle. "This is happening for the rest of your life."

Gabriella groaned while the others laughed.

"Alright, alright," Alicia said. "Ladies, it's time to call it a night. I still have a date tonight with Blake."

"At this hour?" Gabriella said in an incredulous tone.

"Sure. We're so busy throughout the day that the only time we have is at night after Willow has gone to bed."

"Alicia, are you sure we don't need to move up your wedding at this rate?" Jasmine asked. "Ouch, Dana! What was that for?"

"That was on behalf of Alicia. The smack on your head should straighten out the kinks in your thinking," Dana said.

Gabriella chuckled. Those two were a hoot. They must have so much fun as roommates. She yawned—she was exhausted, and it was time to catch some sleep. "Goodnight, everyone," Gabriella said.

"Goodnight," they all echoed, and she ended the call.

Gabriella dropped her phone on the bedside table before lying back down and placing her hands beneath her head.

It'd been nice of the girls to call and congratulate her. It still felt unreal that she was going out with Jason. One minute she'd been at the office, and in the next she'd gotten a call from her friend, rushed to see Jason, and ended up with a boyfriend. Gabriella wasn't sure how everything would turn out, but she planned to enjoy every minute of it.

She dove under the covers and closed her eyes. It was time to sleep.

Gabriella couldn't wait to see how their first day as a couple would play out in the office.

CHAPTER 19

"Good morning!" Gabriella greeted Lacey cheerily before heading into her inner office early the next morning. She removed her spring jacket and hung it on the coat stand before plopping into her chair.

That was when she noticed the big bouquet of red roses on her desk.

Her lips widened into a smile. It had to be Jason. There was a note attached, and she opened it.

Have a fantastic day! With all my love, J, the note read.

Gabriella giggled. This was so sweet. She slipped the note into her bag. Then she picked up the bouquet and inhaled the heady fragrance.

Nice. She could get used to this. Today was indeed a good day.

Lacey knocked on the door, and Gabriella bade her to come in.

Her eyes widened when she saw the bouquet. "Oooh, flowers. But how did they get in here?" she asked as she dropped a stack of files for Gabriella's attention on the desk.

Gabriella shrugged. Jason must have arrived super early and gotten the maintenance folks to open up her office. "Could you find a vase for these?" she said as she handed off the flowers to Lacey.

"Sure thing," Lacey said. She studied Gabriella's face. "Something good must have happened."

"Maybe." The corners of Gabriella's lips turned up in a smile.

"Whatever it is, please please please hold on to it. You're practically glowing."

Gabriella smiled and made no comment. She pulled open her desk drawer and saw the stacks of chocolate and sweets she'd accumulated over time. "Lacey?"

"Yes, Dr. Landi."

"Could you clear out the sweets in my desk drawer later?"

"Wow, now I really want to know what happened to you."

"Hey, it wasn't that bad."

"Yes, it was. You got into them anytime you were worried about something, which meant almost all the time. I got scared that all your teeth would rot or you would get diabetes."

Gabriella's gaze met Lacey's. "I'm sorry."

"I think I might have sand in my eyes," Lacey said as she blinked back tears. Gabriella had no idea she'd worried Lacey so much. "Okay, okay. I'm good. Back to work for me now."

"Thank you," Gabriella said.

"You're welcome." She gave Gabriella a small smile before stepping out of the office and closing the door behind her.

Gabriella leaned back into her custom leather swivel chair, picked up her phone, and sent Jason a text.

Thanks for the flowers, the text read.

There was no immediate response, so Gabriella figured he'd text or call her back later.

She'd only managed to put her bag away

when her desk phone rang. She pressed the speaker button. "What is it, Lacey?"

"Dr. Silvers would like to see you in his office."

Her heart quickened. He was a smooth one alright. Well, she was going to do what *the doctor* ordered. "Thank you, Lacey."

Gabriella got up and headed to Jason's office. The outer office was empty, but she could see the lights shining within. She knocked lightly on the door and entered.

The next thing she knew she was in Jason's arms. "Good morning, Gabriella. How was your night?"

His woody mint-citrus scent enveloped her, and his arms were warm and safe, which was just what she needed. She looked into his eyes. "You?"

"Great. Best sleep in a very long time."

"Me too."

"I've missed you," he said before planting a kiss on her forehead. "Crazy, right?"

"Sort of."

He gave her a light pat on her arm. "Hey."

"Just joking." She leaned her head on his chest. "Thanks for the flowers."

"You're welcome."

"But how did you get the maintenance guy to open my office for you? My office is usually off-limits."

"It's a secret."

"Okay, Secret Man, I need to head back to my office."

"Can't you stay a little longer?"

"Alright. Only for a few minutes, then it's back to work."

The warmth of his arms lulled her into ease, and she settled in further. But then her skin tingled where hers touched his, and her heart rate picked up its beat. She could feel his heart rate quicken as well. Soon hers matched his.

Gabriella's breath hitched, and she swallowed. She wanted to kiss him, but she wished he would kiss her first.

Then his hand touched her jaw and tipped her chin up. Gabriella looked into his eyes and felt drawn in, captivated by the joy and tender care she saw reflected there. His minty breath feathered her cheek.

"Can I kiss you?" he asked softly.

She wanted his kiss, but they were in the office. It would be embarrassing if anyone caught them together, not to mention unprofessional. The woman involved, her in this case, would always be the one blamed. But still, she wanted the kiss. "Yes."

Jason leaned closer, and the butterflies in her stomach began to flutter from his nearness. His right hand splayed across her back and held her steady, the touch sending zaps of electricity coursing through her. The butterflies in her belly began to dance. She reached out her arms and looped them around the back of his neck, bringing his head closer.

Then his lips met hers.

It was soft like the brush of a butterfly's wings at first. His lips tasted sweet, full of goodness and tenderness, and Gabriella wanted more. She deepened the kiss and then he took over, flooding her body with light and all things wonderful. His kiss swept her off her feet and took her away to a universe where only both of them existed.

All too soon, Jason ended the kiss and rested his forehead against hers. "Thank you," he said simply, and Gabriella melted all over again for him. They stayed that way for a moment, lost in their memories.

"Dr. Silvers, oh sorry, I didn't … I'll come back," a familiar voice said.

Gabriella flinched and hid her face. This was so embarrassing. How was she ever going to face Lacey again? She heard his office door close.

"Are you okay?" Jason asked her.

"What are we going to do? Now Lacey knows."

"Would she tell everyone?" Gabriella shook her head. Lacey would never betray her. "Good."

"But how am I going to face her from now on?"

"I think she would make a great ally."

Gabriella looked up at Jason. "What do you mean?"

"Now, we have someone that can help us out if we need to sneak out for a kiss or two," Jason said in a playful tone.

Gabriella punched his arm. "Can you be serious?"

"Ouch, that hurts!"

"I doubt it. But I'm pretty sure you think a kiss would make it all better."

"How did you know?"

"I can read you like a book." She stood on

tiptoe and gave him a soft kiss. "Have a great day, lover boy."

"You too, girlfriend. Did I mention you look fantastic?" Gabriella had dolled herself up in a cream turtleneck paired with a grey pant suit, and her hair bounced in a ponytail behind her.

"Nope. You were more interested in my mouth at the time."

Jason chuckled. "What am I going to do with you?"

"Love me."

"That I can certainly do. Have a good day."

"You too." Gabriella turned and left his office.

She couldn't imagine the rest of her day being much better than this.

"I'm off."

Gabriella looked up from her computer to see Lacey at the door. "It's that time already?"

"Yes. Most folks have left the office."

"Interesting. I still feel so energized."

"Sure, you are. Kissing can do that, you know."

Gabriella's face warmed. "Well, Jason and I are going out."

Lacey's face lit up with joy. "That's wonderful! Certainly better than what's-his-face. He gave me the shivers. Brrr."

Gabriella looked at her in surprise. "Why didn't you tell me?"

"Would you have listened? You were so caught up in that Scott fellow."

"True. But I'm glad that chapter is over."

"Me too. Alright. Don't stay too late. You have a boyfriend now."

Gabriella picked up her phone and checked the screen. "I wonder where the man in question might be."

"Right here," Jason said as he poked his head in.

"Good evening, Dr. Silvers," Lacey said. "And goodnight." She made a quick escape.

Gabriella chuckled. "Come on in."

Jason strode into the room and then leaned against her desk. "Do you still have a lot to take care of?"

Gabriella shook her head. "I'm done."

Jason ran his hand through his hair. "I had no idea this work could be just as tiring as surgery. I have a newfound respect for you doing this day after day."

Gabriella leaned back in her swivel chair. "You don't enjoy it."

"I do, but I miss the surgeries."

Would he be offended if she asked? "Why did you leave surgery? You don't have to answer if you don't want to, but I remember it was all you talked about doing with the rest of your life when we first met many years ago."

Jason stayed silent for a moment. "I needed a change, and your brother offered a chance," he said finally.

Gabriella could tell he was hiding something, but she decided not to push him. Jason would tell her when he was ready. "Okay."

"Are you all set to leave now?" he asked, changing the subject.

Gabriella smiled. "Sure. Give me a minute to pack up my things."

But Gabriella couldn't help wondering what he'd been thinking about that had changed his demeanor.

She hoped it wasn't big enough to affect their newfound relationship.

CHAPTER 20

"Come on in," David said.

Jason entered David's apartment and slumped into the couch.

"It seems you have something on your mind," David said, taking the seat opposite him.

Jason looked at David. "You know me too well."

"What is it?"

"Gabriella asked me tonight about why I'd stopped operating and switched careers."

"And?"

"I couldn't tell her."

"Why?"

"How am I supposed to explain that the incident with her was what triggered the damage that caused the tremors? She'd never forgive herself and might even feel beholden to me. And that's not what I want. I don't want her to stay with me out of guilt. Or she might even think she doesn't deserve to be by my side and leave me."

"But you can't hide it forever. You'll have to tell her at some point."

Jason ran a hand through his hair. "I don't know what to do, man."

"Tell her. Let her find out from you before she hears about it from someone else. Gabriella might just surprise you. She's stronger than you think she is."

"Okay, I'll figure something out."

"Seriously. Tell her sooner rather than later."

Jason wasn't exactly convinced, but what David said made sense. It was better she heard it from him.

He decided he'd tell her the next day.

CHAPTER 21

"Dr. Landi, there's someone at reception to see you," Lacey said as she stepped into Gabriella's office.

It had been a busy day so far especially with the SK101 project moving ahead at full steam. Gabriella had been here since the early hours of the morning and hadn't made it through half of what she'd planned to accomplish today. There had been meetings, more meetings, and yet more meetings. This was her first break since morning, and now someone had come to see her during it.

"Who is it?" Gabriella asked.

"A Ms. Lila Johnson."

Gabriella had never heard the name before. "Does she have an appointment?"

"No, but she said you'd want to see her. That it's about Dr. Silvers."

About Jason? Who could it be? Wait! Was it his mom? No, it couldn't be. The visitor didn't have the same last name as Jason's and Jason's parents were not separated or divorced. So who could it be?"

"Have them send her up, please."

"She said she'd prefer to meet you downstairs," Lacey answered.

This was interesting. Now, her curiosity was piqued. "Tell them I'll be down in five minutes."

"Okay." Lacey left the office.

Gabriella put on her suit jacket, picked up her phone, and stepped out of the office. Two minutes later, she was exiting the elevator on the ground floor. She strode to the reception desk, where a young man was working on a computer. The lobby was almost empty—most employees were still at their desks.

The young man stood to his feet as soon as he saw her. "Dr. Landi."

"Hello, Charles. How are you doing?"

"Fine, Dr. Landi."

"I heard there's someone here to see me."

"She's over there." Charles gestured to the seating area on the far right. A tall woman dressed in an immaculate red suit that fitted her body to a tee sat on the couch and waited with crossed legs. A man in a dark suit stood behind her. Gabriella didn't recognize her, though she looked vaguely familiar. Who could she be?

Gabriella strode to where she sat, her high heels making a *click-clack* sound on the polished marble floor. She soon reached the woman. "Lila Johnson?" she asked. "I'm Dr. Landi, and I've been told you wanted to see me."

The woman rose to her feet and towered over Gabriella. "Unbelievable. A midget?"

Gabriella knew she was petite, but she'd never been called a midget. It seemed this person was only here to insult her, and Gabriella had too much on her plate to entertain this sort of thing. "Have a good day, Lila Johnson." She turned and started back across the lobby.

"Lila?" Jason's familiar voice said. Gabriella halted and turned to see Jason had entered the building. "What are you doing here?"

And just like that, Gabriella remembered where she'd seen Lila. This was *the* Lila Johnson, daughter to the longest serving senator—there were even speculations that he'd run for president in the next election. She looked from Lila to Jason. Had she been the one engaged to Jason?

Gabriella turned to Charles and gestured for him to leave. He nodded and walked outside. Now they were all alone. But she wasn't sure how long it would last before someone exited the elevators.

"It's so good to see you, Jason," Lila purred in a sweet voice. "You look good as always."

By now, a black expression had settled over Jason's face. "I said, what are you doing here, Lila?"

"Hmmm. I wanted to get a glimpse of the girl that's turning your head. She looks different too than in the photo with you."

What picture? Gabriella hadn't snapped any photos with Jason. Unless … she remembered the *click* sound she'd heard at the restaurant. So that had been *her*? Had she had Jason followed? *Yikes.* That was super creepy.

"You have no right to come here," Jason countered. "This is my workplace, and I'd like you to leave now. Or would you prefer to see your photo plastered all over social media? Because that's what's going to happen if any of the other employees see and recognize you."

Lila moved toward the exit with the man in the suit right behind her, but then she halted and turned back. "She doesn't know, does she?"

Gabriella looked from Lila to Jason. Know what? What was she missing?

"Lila, stop—"

"That she's the one that ruined your hands." She turned to Gabriella and pointed at her with a perfectly manicured finger. "You ruined his hands."

Shock rippled through Gabriella. What was she talking about?

"I think you should leave before I call security for trespassing," Jason said.

"Jason!" Lila said.

"I mean it, Lila. Go!"

Lila gave Gabriella a look that burned with hate. "This is not the end." Gabriella stood in shock as Lila whirled around and left through the revolving door before climbing into a black limousine idling in front of the building. The man in black slipped into the front passenger seat, and the limousine drove away.

Jason hurried to where Gabriella stood like a statue.

"Jason, what did she mean?" Gabriella asked in a whisper.

"Gabriella, please—"

"Tell me now, Jason. I need to know. Did I hurt your hands?" Suddenly, she remembered the day they'd run into each other, and she clasped her hand over her mouth. "Was it that day, Jason?" she said in a whisper. "Please."

"Yes, but—"

Gabriella gasped. Her carelessness had ruined his life. If only she'd been paying attention. If only she hadn't ridden a bike that day. She'd destroyed and taken away from him the one thing he'd loved the most.

"Gabriella, you need to listen to me," Jason pleaded.

"I'd like to be alone, Jason. Please."

Gabriella turned and walked away.

Gabriella inhaled deeply as she stood in the rooftop garden at the top of the office building. It had been created as a quiet place for the company's CEO, but her father had never used it, so Gabriella had long since adopted it as her own. It was a great place to clear her head when she had a lot on her mind.

Like today.

She removed the hair tie that held up her ponytail and ran her hands through her hair. So it'd been her all along, the one who messed up. She'd been the one that had made Jason lose the most important thing in his life. How could she look him in the eyes again?

She let out a sigh. What was she going to do now? They couldn't continue the relationship, pretending all was well. How was she going to live with herself? She had more questions than answers, and she didn't know where to turn to.

The door to the rooftop opened. Gabriella looked back to see who had the guts to disturb her in this place. Then she saw David, and her shoulders relaxed. But how had he known she was here?

"Gabriella, I'm so sorry," he said as he strode

over to where she stood and wrapped his arms around her.

As the weight of what she'd done settled on her shoulders, Gabriella let out a small cry and her voice choked with emotion.

"Shh. It's going to be alright." David said as he rubbed his hands up and down her back till her sobs subsided.

She wiped her eyes with the handkerchief he provided. "How did you know I was here?"

"Jason called me."

He still cared about her wellbeing in spite of what she'd done, which made her feel worse. Tears filled her eyes again. "I don't know what to do," she cried out.

"No matter what you decide, you'll be fine," David said. "But, Gabriella, you need to talk to him and hear him out before you make any decisions."

"I know, but it's hard."

"That's what makes us adults, right?"

"I know."

She wiped at her eyes and retied her hair into a ponytail. "Okay, I'll go talk to him. Do you know where he is?"

"Probably wearing out the carpet in his office."

"Thanks, David."

"You're welcome, Ella. Now go."

She squeezed his hand and then left.

It was time to face the discussion she wished she could avoid.

Jason paced up and down his office. Was Gabriella okay? He could only imagine how terrible she felt about what had happened. What if she chose to end the relationship?

His heart hurt just thinking about it. Even though it had only been a few days since they'd started dating, he felt like he'd known her forever, the rib in his side he hadn't known he was missing. He loved everything about her, and even with this situation, he was confident they could work things through if only she gave him a chance.

His relationship with Gabriella was different, the kind he'd never expected to experience in his life. He'd never thought a miracle was possible, but it had happened to him—he, Jason Silvers, had fallen in love.

Because that was what it was. Jason loved his career, but Gabriella mattered more to him. He could trade a million careers in his life just for the chance to be with her. She made him happy, and he found joy in thinking of different ways to make her smile. He'd never dreamed of a wonderful married life before and had accepted an arranged marriage as his destiny, but with her he was looking forward to the future, to settling down, having kids with her, and growing old with her.

But all that wouldn't happen if she decided to break up with him. His heart would probably break from it, but it was better than watching her be miserable.

Because she was all that mattered.

His door opened, and he watched her walk in.

Jason froze and didn't know what to say. His eyes searched her face, and he saw telltale signs that she'd been crying.

Jason felt his heart break a little. He walked

over to where she stood and stopped in front of her. "Are you okay?" he asked.

She nodded, but didn't look him in the eye.

"Please, Gabriella, look at me."

She lifted her eyes, and all he could see was the agony in them.

His heart squeezed a little tighter. "I'm sorry," he said.

She shook her head. "It's all my fault. I did this to you."

He wanted to touch her and reassure her that everything was okay, but he wasn't sure if he could. The last thing he wanted was to make her feel overwhelmed. For now he could only use words, and he prayed she would hear his heart. "You didn't. I had injuries in my wrists before from playing polo many years ago."

"But the biking incident made it worse."

"Maybe, but it could easily have been something else. I even had an MRI after the incident, but the injury didn't show up then. It could have been caused by anything."

"I'm sorry." She reached out and held his hand.

That was all the encouragement Jason needed to pull her into his arms. He wished he could take away the hurt she felt and shoulder it all alone.

He waited till she calmed down and then he said, "Let's sit." He led her to the sofa, and they both sat down. "I need to tell you something," he said.

Gabriella looked at him with those beautiful eyes that made his insides flip. "What?" she asked.

"I know what happened wasn't what we wanted, but I'm glad I met you again, Gabriella Landi. I really, really like you a lot, and I want you in my life. I'm getting therapy for my hands, and who knows? A miracle might still happen. But even if it doesn't, I'm okay as long as I have you in my life. In the worst case scenario, we could continue to work together like this. It's been fun stepping out of my comfort zone, and the stolen kisses aren't bad either."

Gabriella chuckled. "Oh, stop it."

Thank goodness she could smile again. "So what do you think, Gabriella Landi? Should we continue sailing on this ship we're on?"

She gave him a warm smile. "Okay."

"Awesome." He leaned forward and gave

her a soft gentle kiss on the lips. "You're beautiful, you know that?"

"Even with the puffy eyes?"

"Especially with the puffy eyes."

"You're crazy."

"Of course. I'm crazy about you."

"Oh, stop already."

He pulled her back into a hug. "We're going to be fine," he said. And he truly believed it with all his heart.

But a small part of him was worried about the fact that Lila Johnson had come.

Because usually his mother was right behind her.

His phone rang.

CHAPTER 23

Jason sat in the car and looked out at the hospital complex that was Dexington Medical. He'd been coming here for weekly treatments since his leave started, but it wasn't the same. Now, he was entering the hospital not as a patient but as a medical staff.

"You're going to do great," Gabriella said quietly from beside him and squeezed his hand. She'd driven him here after Jason had gotten the call from his department chair, asking for his help with a patient.

Mary Moore, Beth Moore's identical twin sister, had the same surgery that Beth had gone through scheduled for today. The only difference? Mary Moore had anxiety disorder, and she'd had a meltdown as they were about to wheel her into surgery.

When it seemed the only option left was to cancel the operation, Beth had mentioned that Mary might be willing to go in if Dr. Jason Silvers, the surgeon who'd done her own breast reduction surgery, was present. Since Mary had been pleased with Beth's results, she thought Mary might be assured all would go well with her surgery if she saw the same doctor. The hospital had figured it was worth a shot since Jason still had hospital rights at Dexington Medical, and the call had been made.

Jason hadn't expected he'd be back here so soon. The wound was still fresh, and he hadn't had time to prepare his mind for what he was about to experience. But sitting here in the car would do no good. The time had arrived for him to go in. Mary was waiting.

"You'll be fine," Gabriella repeated. "Would you like me to wait for you till you're done?"

"Would you?"

"Of course. I'll just find a parking spot. I have some documents in the car that I can work on while I wait."

"Thanks. I'll see you later."

"See you soon."

Jason took a deep breath, got out of the car, and strode through the revolving doors into the hospital.

Time to get this over with.

Jason entered the surgical attending on-call room and headed to his locker. Fortunately, he hadn't emptied it, so he grabbed a fresh pair of scrubs and changed out of his suit.

His mind whirled as he hung up his clothes in the locker. How would he feel when he entered the OR suite again? Would he experience heartache as he remembered his last surgery or would he be nostalgic as he recalled the good memories he'd made over the years in the OR? But one thing Jason was sure of, regardless of how he felt, his number one priority was making sure Mary made it into the OR.

A few minutes later, Jason held Mary's hand as they wheeled her from the pre-op area into the operating room.

"Am I going to be alright?" Mary asked.

Jason smiled at her. "You'll do great. You're in good hands. Do you have any other questions for me?"

Mary shook her head. "Thank you for coming, Dr. Silvers. I can see why Beth spoke so highly of you."

"My pleasure. The anesthesiologist is going to take over now, but I'll be right here where you can see me before you go to sleep."

"Okay."

Jason nodded to the anesthesiologist that they were ready. The anesthesiologist took over, and soon enough, Jason watched as Mary's eyes closed.

His shoulders relaxed. He was glad everything had gone well.

Jason looked around the OR. He missed this place. Sure, he was only here as a non-sterile staff since he wasn't scrubbed in, but it didn't matter. He missed the sights, the sounds, the smell, everything. He remembered both his first and his last surgery. His heart ached at the loss, but not as much as he'd expected it to.

It was time for the surgeon to come in and start the surgery. Jason took one final look around and left the operating suite. He discarded the head gear, mask, and gloves in the disposal container. Then he walked out of the OR.

A part of him didn't want to leave the surgical wing immediately, so Jason found a corner to sit down and watched the medical staff, patients, and their guardians go about their business. He chuckled when he saw medical students make the same mistakes he made many years ago—talked the ear off another medical student or appeared to be a know-it-all and ignored the advice the nurse was giving him—or when a resident threw out a medical terminology Jason was sure the guardian didn't understand. He recalled memories of his time as a medical student, a resident, and then finally as an attending.

His heart ached as each memory flashed by, but Jason knew it was important that he said goodbye. He'd spent most of his life in the hospital, and even though it was hard to imagine life outside of it, he would create new memories. He'd only ever imagined being a surgeon, so specializing in another area of medicine or becoming a researcher were options he wasn't interested in.

Finally, when he thought it was time, Jason got up, headed to the elevators, and returned to the on-call room. He changed back to his street clothes and headed down to the lobby. With each step, he felt a piece of his heart staying behind, and by the time he made it to the hospital entrance, he was barely holding it together.

But then he looked up and saw Gabriella smiling and beckoning at him from the car she'd parked out front.

His heart eased, and at that moment, Jason knew life would turn out alright.

Everything was going to work out just fine.

Gabriella drove Jason home in companionable silence. Jason stared out the window and watched as cars and houses whizzed by. The ache in his heart was still there, but it would get better with time.

Soon they arrived on Bakers street, and Gabriella parked in front of Jason's town house. She said nothing and just waited for him.

His heart swelled. She understood his need

for silence and had given him the space he needed. *Thank you, God, for bringing this wonderful woman into my life,* he prayed. It was nothing short of a miracle.

Gabriella gave him a warm smile and entwined her fingers with his. Jason raised her hand to his lips and kissed the back of her knuckles. "Thank you," he said.

"Are you okay?" she asked quietly.

"I will be."

"You did great."

"Thank you." He leaned forward and gave her a kiss on the forehead. She was precious, and he would do everything in his power to protect her. "I think I should go in."

"Do you want me to come along?" she asked.

He shook his head. "We both know that's risky," he said with a small smile. "I'm a bit vulnerable right now and won't be able to fend off your moves."

Gabriella chuckled. "You're a rascal, you know."

"Not yet. But I will be if you come in. You don't want to see my rascally side."

"Okay, okay, I'll stay away."

"The angelic side of me thanks you."

Gabriella shook her head in disbelief and laughed. "Can I see you to your door?"

"Sure, as long as you stand ten feet away."

"Okay."

Jason opened the car door and stepped down, then walked around to the driver's side and opened the door for Gabriella.

"Thank you," she said and got out.

Jason led the way to the door. "We're here."

"So soon?" Gabriella asked with a teasing smile.

"Yep. Goodnight, Gabriella."

"Goodnight. You can go inside."

"No, I'll wait for you to leave first."

"Alright." She turned to leave.

"Well, that's a sight," said a voice he'd never expected to hear in Dexington.

Jason looked up and saw his mother walking toward him.

His nightmare had arrived.

CHAPTER 24

Jason turned to Gabriella. "Goodnight," he said. He had to make her leave immediately. This was not the way he'd planned to introduce Gabriella to his mother. He was sure her acerbic tongue would be out in full force. He wondered what nonsensical story Lila had fed her.

Gabriella looked from him to the vision in cream that was his mother. She was willowy, with a face and body that would make princesses jealous. Every strand of her dark-colored hair was in place.

Jason willed her to leave.

Gabriella must have gotten the message

because she gave him a small wave, entered her car, and drove off.

Jason let out a sigh of relief. First crisis averted. This wasn't the best night to deal with his mother, considering what he'd just been through, but he would make do.

"Hello, Mother," he said as he waited for her to reach him. He'd learned from experience that his mother liked to do things at her own pace.

"Hello, Son." She looked at the townhouse in front of them in disdain. "Is this where you're staying?"

"Yes. Would you like to come in?" There was no point asking how she'd gotten his address. His mother had always been able to find him no matter where he went.

"Are you being serious?"

"Yes." She probably thought the place was beneath her.

His mother looked at Jason like he'd grown two heads. "Let's talk in the car," she said.

"Sure."

~

Jason faced his mother as they sat in the back seat of her black limousine. "Mother, why are you here?"

"To stop you from making a big mistake. You're my only son, and I won't allow you to go out with that gold digger."

Jason's nostrils flared. "She's not a gold digger, and I won't allow you to insult her."

"She's not decent enough for you. You need to marry a good girl that won't bring shame to the family."

"Like Lila? Mother, I'm pretty sure you don't really know her." Lila had a wild side to her that he was sure his mother had never seen.

"Lila is a fine girl from a fine family."

Nothing Jason said would change his mother's mind, so he didn't push. But he had no plans to have anything to do with Lila. "She broke up with me, remember?"

"She's seen the error of her ways."

"Are we so desperate? I thought we were old money. Isn't it beneath our family to marry a woman who had rejected your son before?"

His mother's face hardened. "I won't sit here and watch you disrespect our family. Lila's family and ours have been friends for a long time and have been a huge help to us."

"I'm sure that help went both ways. We don't owe them anything. *I* don't owe them anything. Mother, it's time you gave up on this. This is my decision."

"And look where that kind of decision got you. You wanted—no, insisted you would be a surgeon. Now you're a has-been who couldn't open up his own business and had to rely on friends to get a job. Is this what your *great decision* has amounted to?"

That was a punch below the belt, and Jason's heart squeezed in pain. "I think this conversation is enough for tonight, Mother." He jerked open the back seat door. "Have a safe trip back home."

He stepped out and close the door behind him, and waited on the sidewalk till the limousine started and drove off.

Jason straightened his shoulders. This was just the beginning.

He was going to make sure he won, no matter what it took.

CHAPTER 25

Gabriella pulled her pillow over her head as the shrill tone of her phone rang through the air.

"Go away," she mumbled to herself and turned her head away from the bedside table where her phone rested.

But the phone continued ringing.

"Argh." She pulled her head from under the pillow and sat up. Who could be calling her this early? She had tossed and turned all night, courtesy of the shock of seeing Jason's mom, and she was exhausted. The extra time to sleep was what she needed right now.

She picked up her phone and looked at the screen. It was a number she didn't recognize.

Who could it be? She swiped the green button and placed the phone against her ear. "Hello."

"This is Mrs. Silvers," a cultured unfamiliar voice said from the other end of the line.

Mrs. Silvers? Jason's mom? All sleep fled from her eyes. "Good morning, Mrs. Silvers."

"I'd like to meet you now in the coffee shop on Richbridge." Richbridge was two streets away from where Gabriella lived.

"Now?" It was six a.m. Which coffee shop opened at this time?

"Yes, now. I'll be waiting." The line went dead.

Gabriella dropped the phone on the bed and ran her hand through her hair. Should she call Jason and tell him about it? No, it could probably worsen their relationship, and she couldn't be party to that.

It was probably better to hear what Jason's mom had to say first. She could then tell Jason all about it. Besides, his mom seemed the type that would persist till she had her way. It was better to just get it over with as quickly as possible.

Gabriella jumped up from the bed and sprinted into the bathroom.

Gabriella sat opposite Mrs. Silvers in the coffee shop. She'd managed to reach the place within ten minutes. The coffee shop had indeed been open, the smell of fresh bread filled the air, but there were no other customers in sight. It was almost as if his mom had rented out the whole space.

Gabriella waited for her to speak. Her stomach was in knots, but she tried to keep her face as calm as possible. This was Jason's mom, and she had to be careful to treat her right, no matter how terrible Jason's relationship was with her.

Mrs. Silvers finally put down the coffee cup she'd been sipping from.

"So, you're Gabriella Landi."

"Yes, ma'am."

"I believe we met yesterday, but you didn't stop to say hello."

"It was what Jason wished."

"You obey his every command."

"I respect his wishes."

His mom leaned back and studied Gabriella.

"Let me get straight to the point. I need you to leave my son."

"Ma'am, I care for your son very much."

"That's what they all say when all they're interested in is his money."

"I have enough money of my own."

"Right. I've seen the paltry amount. But it doesn't matter what you wish though. You're going to leave my son alone."

"Ma'am, I—"

Jason's mom flung a set of pictures at Gabriella.

Gabriella picked up one and gasped. It was the photo that Scott Sanders had taken. She scanned the others and they showed her in various poses in her underwear. The backdrop seemed to be the restaurant she'd woken up in. How had this happened? "How did you—"

"—get them? You shouldn't have taken them in the first place with your ex-boyfriend." Mrs Silvers leaned forward. "Ms. Landi, I'm not going to let you ruin my son. If you don't break up with him within twenty-four hours, I'm going to release these pictures. You can imagine how your family and colleagues would feel seeing these plastered all over the internet. The decision is yours."

Gabriella's heart sank.

What she'd feared most had finally come true.

CHAPTER 26

Jason took a deep breath and slid the hotel card into the card reader of his mother's suite. Her bodyguard had dropped off the card for him this morning—his mother had instructed that Jason come by and see her as soon as possible.

He'd decided to meet her this morning and talk things through with her. His most important priority was getting her out of Dexington and back to Connecticut. He was willing to give up all his wealth if that was what it took to gain his freedom from his mother. Even though he'd lost his lucrative career, his current job paid more than enough to take care of him and any family he would have, and he had his savings as well.

The door unlocked, and he entered the suite. He heard his mother's voice coming from the direction of the bedroom, like she was talking to someone on the phone. Jason opted to wait till she was done before alerting her to his presence.

He surveyed the room—it was opulent like he'd expected and decorated in shades of gold and browns. His throat suddenly felt dry so he got up and padded to the tray on the dining table where bottles of water rested.

That was when he heard Gabriella's name mentioned.

Gabriella? What had his mother been up to? Jason moved closer to the bedroom to hear what was being said. Luckily, the door was slightly ajar.

"Don't you worry, dear. She's going to be out of his life soon. She has no choice or the pictures will be released." His mother listened to the response on the other end of the line. "But you have to be good this time. I won't have you play games with my son again."

Jason's heart thudded loudly in his chest. What had his mother done to Gabriella? Was that the reason she hadn't picked any of his calls this morning? He'd assumed she was busy with meetings.

His jaw tightened. If his mother had started messing with Gabriella, then it was time to take care of her. He hadn't really wanted to do this, but she'd pushed him to the wall and given him no choice.

But first he had to make sure Gabriella was okay.

She was the most important person in his life, and he couldn't allow anything to happen to her.

CHAPTER 27

Gabriella threw down the pencil she'd been holding. She'd taken the day off after the meeting with Mrs. Silvers, pleading a headache. She'd tried to sketch to take her mind off things, but it wasn't working. The memories of the meeting replayed in her mind over and over again.

Jason's mom hadn't bothered to take the pictures, and they were now stashed in a shoe box at the back of her closet. She would burn them later when she got a chance.

But what was she going to do?

The threat hadn't been idle—Mrs. Silvers seemed the kind of person that would follow through. Gabriella had twenty-four hours to make up her mind.

If Gabriella picked Jason, Mrs. Silvers would release the photos. The pictures would remain a perpetual source of embarrassment for her and her family, and she would lose her job and the chance to be the CEO of Landisil Silicone. She might have to remain in hiding for a while from the media and would eventually bring shame to Jason. In short, her life as she knew it would be over.

If she chose the pictures, she would lose Jason, which would be devastating. She could get through the loss of her job and dreams, but she wasn't certain she could survive the absence of Jason in her life. He'd stolen her heart; losing him could kill her. And the threat of the pictures would still remain out there.

Gabriella bunched her hair in her hands. She was caught between a rock and a hard place.

What was she going to do?

The doorbell chimed throughout the house. Gabriella rose from where she sat. Who could it be? Her mother had taken her father for his physical therapy, so Gabriella was alone in the house. She wasn't expecting anyone.

She strode to the door and looked through the peephole.

Her heart caught in her mouth, and she disengaged the chain lock and opened the door.

"What are you guys doing here?" Gabriella asked as she looked from Jason to Jasmine, and finally, to David.

"We came to save the princess," Jason said. He looked dashing as always in a beige military style jacket over a blue button-down shirt and jeans.

"What are you talking about?"

"Let's come in first," David said and pushed his way past Gabriella. Jasmine and Jason followed suit. "What about Mom and Dad?"

"Mom took Dad for his physical therapy appointment. Aren't you all supposed to be at work?"

"This was an emergency," Jasmine said as she sat on the custom-sized brown leather couch. David planted himself beside her while Jason took the two-seater.

"What's going on?" Gabriella asked as she plopped down on the remaining seat.

"You tell me," David said. 'What's going on?"

"I don't understand," Gabriella said as she looked from Jasmine to David and finally, to Jason.

"You met my mother," Jason said.

Shoot! How had he found out? There was no way his mother would have informed him. At least, not until she'd gotten the response she was expecting.

"You should have told me," Jason said. "Aren't we in this together?"

Gabriella looked into his eyes and saw the hurt there. "I'm sorry."

"Come here."

She got up and walked over to where he sat. He pulled her beside him on the sofa and hugged her. "Everything is going to be alright," he said. "I won't let anything or anyone hurt you."

"Tell me what happened," David said quietly.

Gabriella shared the conversation she'd had with Mrs. Silvers and mentioned the pictures.

"How could your mother threaten my sister?" David said to Jason.

"I'm sorry."

"Guys, we need to come up with a solution," Jasmine said. "That's what's most important now."

"Do you think we could see them?" David asked.

"I don't know," Gabriella said. "Even though you're my brother, they're still pretty embarrassing, and I don't want to show *him*." She gestured to Jason.

"Honey, there's nothing we three haven't seen," Jason reminded her. "We're all doctors, remember? I think we've seen more nude bodies than any other profession."

"I have an idea and seeing the pictures might help," Jasmine said.

"Okay." Gabriella got up and soon returned with the photos. She handed them over to Jasmine.

Jasmine looked through the pictures one after the other and handed the ones she'd seen to David and then to Jason.

Gabriella watched David's face harden, and

Jason looked like he might burst an artery. "I told you they were horrible."

"I'm mad that these pictures were taken without your consent," Jason said. "I think we should sue the restaurant."

"I agree," David said. "How could they let this happen? It would have taken a while for Sanders to take these pictures. What were the waiters doing?"

"Guys, let's focus here," Jasmine said. "I think we have a plan that might work."

"What is it?" Gabriella asked.

"Let's release them."

"What do you mean release them?" Gabriella said. "That's exactly what I don't want."

"You don't understand. We can turn this into a 'Before and After' campaign for an IntimiRose bra."

"What do you mean?"

"These pictures can become the 'Before' photos. The underwear you have on here are quite bland, sorry to say, so they're perfect. We can then take 'After' photos with you all dressed up in IntimiRose lingerie. We would make it seem like a deliberate marketing campaign for the venture."

"That sounds like a brilliant idea." David gave Jasmine a kiss on the cheek. "You're a genius. What do you think, Ella?"

"I don't know," Gabriella responded. "I'm not sure how I feel about lingerie pictures."

"These photos are going to be released eventually," Jasmine said. "If not today, then sometime in the future. This is an opportunity for us to control how the world *perceives* these pictures. We'll make sure the pictures turn out beautiful and modest."

"And it would remove the threat of these photos once and for all," David said.

Jason placed his hand over Gabriella's. "It's going to be alright."

Jasmine seemed really confident about the strategy, and the others agreed with the plan. Maybe she was overthinking this. "But what about the IntimiRose photos? Mrs. Silvers only gave me twenty-four hours, and the time is already ticking down."

"Leave that to me," Jasmine said.

~

The advertising campaign was a hit. The fact that Gabriella was a company executive heightened its appeal, and the lingerie that Gabriella wore in the 'After' photos sold out within three hours. The demand for Landisil-Silicone products surged, and Gabriella received calls to appear on national TV talk shows, which she declined—the current publicity was more than enough for her.

David had been right. The pictures lost their power over her life.

Mrs. Silvers had been enraged, and after a behind-closed-doors meeting with Jason, had returned to Connecticut. Jason must have had a good heart-to-heart discussion with her, because it seemed she wasn't going to be back anytime soon, for which Gabriella was grateful.

Her parents found out what had really happened with the pictures, but they were both just thankful she was safe.

Everything had worked out, and Gabriella had peace once again.

Now she could focus on her primary objective—winning the CEO seat.

CHAPTER 28

J ason inhaled the fresh spring air as he stood in the rooftop garden and looked out over the city. The setting sun cast a beautiful orange glow to the buildings as it descended for the night.

Though Gabriella didn't know, Jason had also adopted the garden for his own. It was truly an oasis in the midst of a busy city.

Now that the whole picture debacle was behind them, Jason knew the CEO position was all Gabriella was thinking about. She'd accepted that he was running for the job as well and hadn't tried to sabotage or undercut him in any way. But he knew her fear still remained that she might lose, even though she'd been with the company since the beginning and had worked hard as a founding member to bring the company to where it was today. Only a few could claim that accomplishment at so young an age.

As the man who loved her with all his heart, he had to do his best to remove that fear.

He knew just what to do.

Jason picked up the phone and made a call.

"Don't remove the blindfold," Jason said.

"Where are we going?" Gabriella asked as she held onto Jason's arm.

"Just a few more steps. Good. Stop. You can now open your eyes."

Gabriella slid down the blindfold, and her eyes widened. "Jason, why are we at an airport?"

Jason took both her hands in his. "Gabriella, I know the past few days have been very stressful, and I wanted to give you a chance to relax. Welcome aboard Big Bird."

"Big Bird? Isn't that a character on one of those long running children's shows?"

Jason shrugged. "I liked the name, and it suits my jet just fine."

"Your jet?"

"Yes. Mine. Perks of old money."

"Hmmm. He looks cute."

Jason laughed. "First time I've heard him being described as cute."

"So where are we going?"

"Paris."

"What? But I don't have my passport."

Jason pulled a passport from the inner pocket of his jacket. "It's right here. I took the liberty of asking your parents for it."

"We are coming back tonight, right?" She couldn't afford to take the whole weekend off.

"Sure. Unless you don't want to. Gabriella, get those dirty thoughts off your mind."

"Hey, I was just asking. I'm good."

Jason chuckled. "Okay, let's go."

The flight into Paris was uneventful. Gabriella had slept for most of the flight and had woken up feeling refreshed. She met the pilot, co-pilot, and flight attendant, all of whom had worked for Jason for quite some time.

Gabriella turned to Jason once the flight attendant left. "Where are we going in Paris?"

"I thought you might appreciate the Louvre."

"Nice!" She'd always wanted to go and visit the world's largest museum, but she'd never found time to get away. "But won't it be crowded?"

"I've arranged a private tour. The Louvre would already be closed down to the general public."

Gabriella let out a sigh of relief. She was a semi-extrovert, but she hated large crowds, and it would have taken away some of the enjoyment of the place.

The jet landed at the Paris Orly airport, and soon Gabriella and Jason were in a limousine headed to the museum. They arrived within twenty minutes at its main entrance, with the glass and metal pyramid I.M. Pei had designed.

"This is stunning," Gabriella remarked as they got out.

"It's very popular too. It's usually crowded

and hard to get through when the museum is open."

"Have you been here before?"

"Yes, but usually alone. It's different coming here with you."

Gabriella reached out and held his hand in hers. "You always have sweet words."

Jason took her arm and looped it with his. "Do I? I guess it's true."

Gabriella laughed. What was she going to do with this man?

"Welcome to The Louvre Museum." A blonde petite lady had reached them. "My name is Juliette, and I'll be your tour guide for tonight. Shall we?"

"Nice meeting you, Juliette," Jason said. "I'm Jason, and this is Gabriella. Lead the way."

Their audio guide led them first to the Pavillon de l'Horloge. "This is the origin of the museum. It shows what the Louvre looked like when it was first a medieval fortress, and then a twelfth century castle and home to the kings of France, before it became a museum in seventeen ninety-three."

Gabriella looked around. "This is amazing."

"I agree," Jason commented. "I feel like I've stepped back in time."

"These remains were found when the Louvre was extensively renovated." They walked around for a few more minutes, studying and commenting on everything. The conversation was refreshing.

"Why don't we move on to our next stop?" Juliette asked. "The museum has two large wings, the Denon and Richelieu wings, and one smaller Sully wing that connects the larger wings to one another. I'm assuming you'd like to focus on the Denon wing, correct?"

"Can't we see all three?" Gabriella asked.

"It would take more than a full day to go through the whole museum," Jason said. "We could always come back and visit the others."

"I'd like that."

"Great. Let's go with the Denon wing," Jason said to Juliette.

"Perfect. This way."

Juliette led them toward the Denon entrance. "This wing houses the famous *Mona Lisa*. You'll also find Italian and Spanish paintings, large scale French paintings, and Roman sculptures and antiquities."

They entered the ground floor, the Galerie Michel Ange which showcased Italian master-pieces by the likes of Michelangelo and Giambologna. Then they climbed the grand staircase at the end of the gallery, past the *Winged Victory of Samothrace*, a marble monu-ment with incredible details that Gabriella appreciated.

They soon reached the first floor where the paintings section was housed. They walked through the Grand Galerie, an impressive hall filled with exquisite Italian paintings. Gabriella examined *The Seasons*, a series of four paintings created by Giuseppe Arcimboldo in fifteen sixty-three, that used a combination of plants, fruits, and vegetables associated with each season. They also passed *Le Portement de la Croix* by Biagio d'Antonio, a religious painting that depicted the love and despair between Jesus and his mother on his way to the cross. Then they entered the room where Leonardo da Vinci's famous *Mona Lisa* was housed behind protective glass.

"I'd like a picture with the Mona Lisa in the background," Gabriella said.

"We can do that," Jason responded. He

pulled a camera from his jacket and handed it over to Juliette, who took a couple of shots before returning the camera to Jason. "Thank you," he said.

"You're welcome," Juliette replied.

They walked through other halls that housed an impressive collection of large scale French paintings and then Spanish paintings. Jason and Gabriella also visited the Apollo Gallery where they admired the breathtaking fresco ceilings and the famous *Crown of Louis XV*.

Soon, Gabriella began to tire, and Jason suggested they stop here for the night. They thanked Juliette and then exited the museum. They crossed the Arc de Triomphe du Carrousel and entered the Jardin des Tuileries, the fifty-seven acre royal gardens of a former palace, one of the largest urban gardens in the world.

"This reminds me of a super-sized version of the rooftop garden back at the office." Gabriella said.

"It's perfect, right?" Jason said.

"Yes, it is. Perfect ending to a perfect evening."

They found a place to sit and watched the sunset. Gabriella leaned her head on Jason's shoulders. This was such a wonderful gift Jason had given her, and she'd loved every minute of it.

Then Jason turned to her. "Gabriella, the first time I met you, you were this spunky little kid. You were so full of life and brought joy wherever you went. I'm so glad I got the chance to meet you again and fall in love with the woman you have become."

Gabriella's heart pounded in her chest. Was Jason doing what she thought he was doing?

"I love you, Gabriella Landi. You're smart and funny and you laugh at my weird jokes."

"They're definitely weird," Gabriella chimed in.

Jason chuckled. "Don't worry. I have more for you." Then he turned serious. "For the first time in my life, I can picture spending the rest of my life with someone and growing old together. I know you love your rooftop garden, so I figured there was no better place than here to pop this question."

Jason went down on one knee and pulled out a black box from his jacket. He opened it to reveal a beautiful sparkling diamond ring.

Gabriella gasped. It was really happening.

"Dr. Gabriella Landi, would you marry me?"

Gabriella stared into the eager eyes of the man that had stolen her heart. He understood her, loved her, and cherished her.

She knew with all her heart what her response would be. "Yes," she said.

Jason swept her up in his arms and spun her around amidst clapping from the other visitors in the garden.

Then he set her down. "I have one more gift," he said.

He pulled out a smaller flat rectangular box and handed it to her. "Go ahead. Open it."

Gabriella flipped it open to see a folded sheet of paper in it. She pulled it out and unfolded it.

Her jaw dropped as she read the note. "Are you serious?"

"Very much so," Jason replied.

Tears filled her eyes. He'd given her the most unexpected gift. Jason had chosen to drop out of the race for the CEO position, and this was a note from the board accepting his request.

"You didn't have to do that," Gabriella said, even as she brushed away the tears that stained her cheeks.

"I know, but I love you enough to do it."

And Gabriella knew without a doubt that she'd come home.

Their engagement ran in the papers the next day.

Gabriella had protested about the publicity when Jason raised the subject, but he'd insisted it was a strategy that would deter his mother from interfering any further in their relationship.

So she'd let it go. She was happy with how her life had turned out.

Her one-time crush had become her lifelong love.

"Gabriella, you'll wear out the carpet," Jason said.

"I'm sorry," she said and sat down on the couch in her office. But then Gabriella got up again.

Jason chuckled. He totally understood how she was feeling. The board members had met today to decide who the new CEO of Landisil Silicone would be. Even Gabriella's father had made an appearance.

The door opened, and Lacey walked in. Gabriella rushed over to her. "How did it go?" she asked.

Lacey's shoulders slumped. "I'm so sorry—"

Gabriella's heart deflated. "It's okay," she

said. "Jason, thanks for all your support even if it didn't work out." Jason had helped her draw up a strategy that demonstrated how competent Gabriella was in leading the company and had spoken to as many board members as possible on her behalf.

"—that you're going to work twice as hard as the new CEO of Landisil Silicone!" Lacey finished.

"Wait! What?" Gabriella said.

"You're the new CEO, darling," Jason said with a smile.

"Oh my goodness."

"You got sixty percent of the vote, while Foster had forty percent," Lacey added.

"Congratulations, darling," Jason said. "You did it."

Gabriella didn't know what else to say.

Her dream had finally come true.

And she had the best man in the world to share it with.

～

"Hey, Doc, what's going on?"

Jason had received a call from Dr. Meade's

office to come in and see him. He'd brought Gabriella along, and they both waited for Dr. Meade to speak.

Gabriella squeezed Jason's arm. Whatever the news was, they would weather it together.

"Dr. Silvers, how do your hands feel?"

"Okay." Jason had attended all his treatments. Both hands seemed to have improved, but the tissue damage in the right hand still remained. Gabriella had encouraged Jason to consider turning his left into his dominant hand. He'd started working on it, but he still had a long way to go. There was also no guarantee it would ever be good enough for surgery.

"Have you practiced your surgical skills in recent times?" Dr. Meade asked.

"Not really. I didn't want to attempt anything that would jeopardize the treatment. What's going on, Dr. Meade?"

"Well, that's a mistake, because all the tissue damage in your right hand is gone."

Jason stiffened and then swallowed. "What are you saying?"

Dr. Meade's face widened into a smile. "Your right hand looks as good as new. We checked multiple times, and everything looks great. Even the strength testing showed your right hand is stronger than ever before. Congratulations, Dr. Silvers. You got your miracle. It's time to return to the OR."

Jason choked back a cry. Gabriella rubbed his back even as tears filled her eyes.

Jason had finally come to terms with his loss and had even started a 'Surgeons Anonymous' group, where former surgeons who'd had to give up their career for one reason or another got together each month and encouraged each other. The group had been well-received, and even Dexington Medical had reached out to indicate their interest in getting involved.

But God had chosen to be gracious.

To her very own Billionaire Boss Doc.

Thank you so much for reading! Want to know what happens next in Dexington, and how Becca, Jasmine's aunt finds love with a billion-aire cowboy doctor (an amnesia second chance romance)?

Check out LOVING THE BILLIONAIRE COWBOY DOC at https://dobidaniels.com.

Here's an excerpt:

"Not a problem," he said in a deep voice with a faint western drawl that tickled her senses. Truth be told, she could have listened to it all day. Then he gave her a faint smile.

That was it. Becca's heart took off to the races. That smile shone a light on her that warmed her from head to toe and wrapped her in its blanket. She noticed how attractive he was with his solid yet lean build, short sun-kissed hair, and a chiseled symmetrical jawline that was perfect for the cameras. His black rimmed glasses, in contrast, gave him a somewhat geeky look she found adorable. But it was his piercing blue eyes that drew her in—warm, expressive, and so full of light yet with a hint of vulnerability.

Becca averted her eyes. What was she doing? She'd just had her heart broken, and she didn't need another entanglement in her life. It was probably best to just mind her business and leave when she was done.

But her eyes were drawn to his hands that

played with the edge of his hat. These were hands that were no stranger to hard work, with their calluses, yet she could imagine them…

Want to read more? You can grab LOVING THE BILLIONAIRE COWBOY DOC at https://dobidaniels.com!

Or want to know what happens next in Dexington?
Sign up now at https://dobidaniels.com.

If you've loved reading Loving the Billionaire Boss Doc, Dobi would be grateful if you could spend a few minutes to leave a review (as short as you like) on the book's page on your favorite retailer. Your review would help bring it to the attention of other readers. Thank you very much.

Check out all Dobi Daniels books at https://dobidaniels.com

ACKNOWLEDGMENTS

Writing a book is harder and more rewarding than I could have ever imagined. And it would not have been possible without the support, love, and encouragement from my number one cheerleader, my dearest mom. My life would never have been this awesome and wonderful without you.

Of course, I have to thank my precious little DC for his smiles and antics. You brighten my day and give me the strength to keep pushing through.

Thank you to my sisters for encouraging me on this wonderful journey. And a special thanks to my baby brother (who is so not a baby anymore) for being super supportive and checking in on my progress. You guys are the best.

Thank you to my wonderful author friends. You know who you are. Your selflessness and willingness to share what you know has made my writing journey smoother and an exciting one. And a special thanks to Lisa and Deanna whose support have made a difference.

Most of all, I want to thank God who gave me life, surrounded me with the most wonderful people, and loved me all the way. You make my life complete.

And finally, a special thanks to all my readers whose love of my stories spur me on to write more. Thank you!

As a former physician and business executive in another life—with a childhood filled with reading multi-genre novels—Dobi Daniels loves to write sweet thrilling romance stories with heart. She enjoys dreaming up everyday characters who rise above unfavorable circumstances to overcome incredible odds and find joy along the way.

When not writing, Dobi can be found binging K-dramas and ice cream with her little sidekick by her side.

Loving the Billionaire Boss Doc is the fourth book in the Dexington Doctor Billionaires Series. Sign up at dobidaniels.com to be notified when the next Dobi Daniels book comes out!

Thank you!

https://dobidaniels.com
hello@dobidaniels.com
facebook.com/dobidaniels
bookbub.com/profile/dobi-daniels
instagram.com/dobidaniels